The Wish Dog

Other short fiction anthologies available from
www.honno.co.uk

All Shall Be Well
Coming Up Roses
Cut on the Bias
Laughing Not Laughing
My Cheating Heart
My Heart on My Sleeve
Safe World Gone
Written in Blood

The Wish Dog

Haunting Tales from Welsh Women Writers

Edited by Penny Thomas and Stephanie Tillotson

HONNO MODERN FICTION

Published by Honno
'Ailsa Craig', Heol y Cawl, Dinas Powys, South Glamorgan, Wales,
CF64 4AH

1 2 3 4 5 6 7 8 9 10

A catalogue record for this book is available from The British Library.

Published with the financial support of the Welsh Books Council.

ISBN 978-1-909983-09-0

Cover image: Shutterstock
Cover design: Graham Preston
Text design: Elaine Sharples
Printed by Bell & Bain Ltd, Glasgow

Contents

"Is there anybody there?"

What makes a good ghost story? When we first discussed publishing a new anthology of ghost stories by women from Wales, we had no idea what would come to haunt us. We hoped that others would share our fascination with the 'evocative and the eerie', with 'the shiver induced by the thunder of a black, stormy night', could imagine being held spell-bound by a mysterious and, perhaps, macabre tale as the clock strikes midnight: the hour when all light has been extinguished and we poor mortals are most acutely aware of our human limitations. Might not the dead come back to glide silently across our paths, or to scream out of the walls, demanding justice or revenge?

'Is there anybody there?' is a question that most of us have asked at some point or another. The question lies at the kernel of all good ghost stories – and in this collection the unknown answers back! All the tales raise the possibility that we do not finish in eternal silence, that there may be a mysterious purpose to life's arbitrary unfairnesses and disappointments. That there may even be the chance of reunions with those we have loved and lost – or the possibility that we are not to blame for our failings, that there are indeed powerful, sometimes malignant forces that shape our destinies.

So we keep on being fascinated, drawn to poke into our imagination's darkest corners, where we keep thoughts that have no place in our daylight worlds. Let such fears surface and we might struggle to function. Yet, when repressed, our imaginations bubble and boil and another world rises through the floorboards of our daily lives. And so writers continue to question their darker instincts: 'Is there anybody there?'

You may be of a more sceptical nature. Perhaps for you ghost stories are all flapping sheets and *Scooby Doo*. Fun and occasionally scary but holding nothing of any allure. Maybe you prefer the supernatural setting of fairy tales peopled by snow queens and wild swans. Remember though that you can't have such fascinating creatures without the wicked witches and dangerous beasts that come along with them, lurking at the edge of the seductive dream.

What then turns a bunch of clichés into truths that touch the core of our deepest hopes and fears? What makes a *good* ghost story? We offer just one suggestion – pick up this book and read on.

We hope you will discover intriguing stories of the weird and wonderful. They are all surprising, thrilling, full of suspense and very different each from the other. We think there will be something here to satisfy all tastes: from the beautiful, poignant and tender to the downright horrific. These are stories that will take you to somewhere else, maybe just a stone's throw away. Here are crumbling old houses, gothic to their core, such as the mansion of *I, King*, with its Miss Havisham-style rotting fruit, its elusive but open door, appearing suddenly when least expected, always beckoning at the end of a line of trees. Here is the atmospheric: the oppression of heat as beautifully created in *Ants* and *Shade*, the eerie cold of *The Pull of the North*, the significance of *Seashells*. Every slight flicker in the ambience takes on a new import as you read, offers glimpses that may tempt you to look over your shoulder, just for a moment… Here are stories that present, to quote Henry James (a past master of the form), 'The strange and sinister embroidered on the very type of the normal and easy.'

Many, inevitably, work around loss, facing life's tragedies, as in *Broad Beach* and *The View From Up Here*. Here the voices of the dead yearn to teach the living lessons about life, the mystery that is *The Girl in the Grass,* the call for humanity and justice in *The Soldier's Tale* and a *Matter of Light.* There are also the outrageously funny – the bawdy melodrama of *Sovay, Sovay* and the downright naughtiness of *Ghosts*. And, yes, there are even flapping sheets in *Making Ghosts,* a tightly wound tale that subverts conventions, reminding us that we are as numerous as the blades of grass on the great plains; like the one grain of sand on a broad beach that even so cannot exist without its singularity.

A word of warning though: watch your step, much may not be as it seems in this anthology. There are unreliable narrators, apparently friendly guides, who may take you by the hand and lead you onto treacherous ground. Should we trust the narrators of the gloriously crafted *The Wish Dog* and *Caretakers*? And it is only ever a short distance to what we may call madness, touchingly and hauntingly evoked in stories such as *Mad Maisy Sad* and *Convention is the Mother of Reality*.

Preparing this book, what mattered most was not which secret of the otherworldly our authors chose to conjure for us, but the dexterity (even sleight of hand) with which they exposed it. Whether your taste is for fireside shivers or for the exploitation of the 'other side', a few words perfectly placed, a theatrical incantation, or a glut of gothic adornment, this collection offers so much that is wonderfully and entrancingly told. In *Harvest* there is even a haunting, primordial myth promising a terrifying end for those who live for language, stories and the telling of them.

But I think we may have said too much; it will be light soon and you've not begun to read yet…

Penny Thomas and Stephanie Tillotson

Sovay, Sovay

Chrissy Derbyshire

You seem surprised to see me sitting in your chair. I suppose that's why you're brandishing a poker. And may I say how dashing you look, haloed in firelight, all black and flaming red? Why ruin the tableau by doing anything so boorish as bashing my head in?

Quite right. A gentleman never brains a lady with a poker. Besides, it would hardly work. I'm a ghost, you see. Hence, breaking and entering without the breaking. I turned my body into smoke and snaked through your keyhole to haunt you, beautiful. Because I want you. No, not like that. And by the way an *incubus* is a *male* demon. I suspect you mean, *succubus*.

I want you for an audience. I want you for an eager ear. My name was Sovay, and I have such stories. You'd never believe them if I told them a thousand times, and that's fine with me because I can't say they're all entirely true. Some are. Most are. Most of what I say is almost entirely true, minus embellishments and outright lies. You look confused. Perhaps I should start at the beginning.

I am an aesthete, and a sensualist. Where you see the fire, I see blazing colours of sheer, hot light, breaking and sparking against a deeper black. I see welcome warmth against glowing, goosebumped skin. I see demons and salamanders. That is what I see. Perhaps I'm shallow. It's been said, and no doubt if I am remembered it will be said again. And yet I think I can see deeper than most, when I want to, when I can be bothered. The best I can say for you, whoever you are, is that I love you as I love my favourite book. And like my favourite book, it is the little details of you that excite me – deftly written turns of being that titillate and challenge.

Even the love of study is aesthetic, if not carnal. When I read bold or wise ideas that fit so beautifully into place in my mind, it is a secret thrill. The thrill is silent, wispy as a cobweb, caught between the pages of a secondhand book. All my knowledge of the world, I am sorry to say, is aesthetic, fragmentary and insubstantial – a series of imagined sights, smells or touches lingering around my tremulous body and gaspingly sensual mind.

So. You have been warned. I'm not an amoral Dorian Gray or a solipsistic Humbert Humbert (yes, while I was haunting you I also read your books – I hope you don't mind) but I'm still waist-deep in my senses and my imagination when you think I'm listening. And, though I only ever committed one act of violence in my short life, I fear I may somehow still be a little dangerous.

My mother was an actress with the *Grand Guignol.* She was beheaded every night. A consummate professional, she never missed a performance. I was born on stage to a headless woman, and the audience applauded. She paid me little attention but once, in a fit of drunken motherly affection, passed me her wealthy dead grandmother's locket. I never took it off. I wasn't schooled – not in the commonplace sense – but I grew up in the wings and dusty backrooms of the theatre in Pigalle, and I saw enough. The myths about that place are true. The boxes had the air of a confessional. It had been quite a different place of worship before it was transformed into a shrine to bloody violence. Two great angels still presided over the scenes of rape and murder on the stage, blessing every assassination with impassive grace. Luckily they never peeked, as I did, into the boxes. There, respectable folk would re-create the actors' poses in various states of sweaty undress. I never saw anyone beheaded there, but I did see many a gentleman with his head quite hidden under a lady's skirts. When I wasn't snooping and exploring and pilfering pretty things from ladies' bags, I was reading. This and that, novels, playbills, anything I could find. They called me *la gosse Grand Guignol* – the Grand Guignol brat – and I spent my nursery years climbing round the gothic architecture like a dirty-faced spider.

So I grew, half-feral but indiscriminately well-read, until one day it became clear that under the dirt I had grown into an attractive young woman. Not beautiful. Gap-toothed and a little coarse, but with the brightest eyes... Of course...you can see. I was given a play script and measured for a costume – just a simple inmate's gown, coarse on my naked skin. I was to be a young lunatic, mostly cured and soon to leave the asylum. I was pale, red-lipped, cheeks modestly rouged. Every bit the innocent who might be made a victim. My role was not a profound one. I was to talk meekly to the nuns and to the doctors, making my eyes round and sweet like marbles. Then I was to be accosted by two grotesque shrews – fellow madwomen, but not so near curing and with faces like storybook witches – who put out my marble eyes with scissors as punishment for my beauty. The blood-rigged scissors fascinated me. I was scolded time and again for stabbing dolls and apples just to watch the inanimate things gush blood.

Really, none of this is important. History hasn't remembered me. Not even when I changed my given name – Anne-Laure – to Sovay. I named myself for the heroine of that strange English folk song.

Sovay, Sovay, all on a day,
She dressed herself in man's array.
With a brace of pistols at her side,
To see her true love away she'd ride.

The romance of it! She dressed as a highwayman and challenged her lover to stand and deliver. When he refused to give up the ring she'd given him as a love token, she knew she had no need to shoot him stone dead. I always kept a small gun on my person in those days. When you're a pretty young thing who makes eyes at the audience and then bleeds from those eyes all over the stage, people tend to think they own you. A gun in the back is a fair deterrent. 'Those days…' I say, as if I ever passed twenty.

So how would I characterise the genre of this piece? Let us call it a gothic romance. Even better, a 'penny dreadful' with a romantic bent. I'm trying to define it in a way you'd understand. If you were there… Oh, if you were there, in my little palace of violence, all I'd need to say would be that it is pure *Grand Guignol.* Picture the scene: a young actress, still in costume and make-up, steps out into the cold Paris air. It is a strange, smoky night in November. She is bored. The thrills of the night's entertainments have paled, and all at once she must feel the chill pavement under her feet and the gritty walls under her hands. The sky is touched with light, fool's gold of stars and a milk-pale moon swathed in cloud. Somewhere there is music, an owlish mezzo-soprano from a high bedroom. And she steps, and she steps, on and on, and it's like a scene from Perrault – or a dream.

That was the quality of light and sound, and those were the textures of the night that night. I nodded my head to a woman even more painted than I, lounging in a doorway. This was the right side of town for painted ladies. The wrong side of town for everything else. I was contemplating climbing the walls as I had as a child, itching for any kind of adventure, when I saw him.

He was a gentleman. Like you, but where you are still curled in on yourself like a startled anemone – honestly, you'd think you were the first man ever to be haunted – he lounged in the window of the Café de la Paix like he'd never been frightened in his life. Like the lad who couldn't shiver, he reclined in his chair with a glass of something golden and surveyed the thronging post-opera crowd with mild, ironic fascination. He was alone. It was impossible to imagine him any other way. His hair was lush and dark but, in the yellow light of the café, it shone like flax spun to gold. No, really, it did. Of all the things I've told you, *that* is what you question?

All this time I stood barefoot on the cold ground outside the café. To enter would be unthinkable, even with all my actor's nerve. These were opera-goers. They shouldn't even have been in Pigalle otherwise. The entrance of a white-faced ragamuffin in a hospital gown would have caused a panic. So I watched, my breath steaming the glass like a child's who stands gazing at richer children's toys. I watched him watching them. Then his head inclined just a little towards me. His eyes grew wide for a moment – I still had a little blood around mine – and then he smiled broadly, amused and approving, with a little quirk of his eyebrow. He rose and left the café, still holding his glass. Nobody stopped him.

A change of backdrop, then, for the figure suddenly stealing my mind's stage. Against the fantastic gold of the café he had been careless and debonair. Now, against the night, he was a beast. Smiling like one who'd already won the game six moves ahead, he put his glass to my lips and poured the wine down my throat. It tasted like pictures I'd seen of the world beyond Pigalle, beyond Paris. I was in love. When he took me in an alley, both of us still mostly clothed, it was the nearest I'd ever come to romance. Held in his panting, post-coital embrace, I said, 'My name's Sovay.'

'Sophie?'

'Sovay.'

'Well, and why not?' He smiled a droll smile. 'If a courtesan can't choose her name, what *can* she choose?'

'I'm not a whore. I'm an actress.'

'Of course you are. And may I say, your act has quite enchanted me.'

'What's your name?'

'Patrice Follet.'

'I love you, Patrice Follet.'

'And I would love you again tomorrow, Sovay the actress.'

I smiled. It was enough. You see, despite all I'd seen, I'd barely lived. Impulsively I unfastened my locket and pressed it into his sweaty hand. Twelve days later it would be returned to me by a dead man. But I'm getting ahead of myself.

We had many trysts. I introduced him to my theatre. I put out his eyes with the stage-blood scissors and he laughed till he cried, his tears mingling with the red. Bloody nuisance brat, scowled my mother, long since relegated to unofficial accountant and understudy hag. Patrice's fearlessness charmed me. Love is a man who can handle horror with a smile.

I can't say whether there was a catalyst, a particular sight, sound, scent or emotion that caused me to take up the mantle of my namesake. All I can say is that, once the idea took hold, it wouldn't let go.

Patrice was a creature of habit. I knew his movements. It would be easy, so easy, to catch him unawares somewhere quiet. Our very romance testified to his talent for finding shady spots with no witnesses. The clothes were no problem – I pilfered them from the theatre. I bound my breasts with cloth and donned the clothing of a rake. Damned attractive, too. I very much admired myself as a man. My hair I hid under a hat, and a mask obscured the top half of my face. My lips – he'd never seen them unpainted. I loaded my gun for authenticity's sake, and went to find my love.

The moment I stepped out in front of him, I knew something was wrong. The careless smile was gone. Patrice was trembling. Patrice was frightened. I watched with distaste as, his face a picture of pathetic dread, he emptied his pockets of gold. It spilled to the ground, a little puddle around his feet. Righteous disappointment flooded me, painting my cheeks, narrowing my eyes. 'Anything else?' I demanded, making my voice coarse. 'That's not all. Any tokens from your sweetheart?'

With depressing swiftness he put a hand inside his jacket and pulled out the locket. It dangled flimsily from his white-knuckled fist. 'Yes, forgive me,' he said, 'I forgot.'

Oh, I hated him now. My lad who couldn't shiver was a yellow coward when faced with what he perceived to be real danger. Pitiful. Still, I had to give him this one chance. 'Or perhaps,' I said, slowly, significantly, as one might to a foolish child, 'this trinket is too dear to part with.'

'No indeed,' he stammered, dropping the thing on the ground with the coins. 'Just a present from a tart in Pigalle. Worth something to you though, I should think. Real gold. Don't hurt me.'

And so I fulfilled my destiny. I was born into illusion, violence and blood. That night, masked, with a gun in my hand, I claimed my birthright. The shot was clean, through the head. He stood for a moment like a great, gross puppet, then crumpled to the ground. Real blood is a lusher, more nuanced red than stage blood, I noticed. I felt detached, like a ghost already. I took the locket, left the money, and walked back to the theatre.

I shan't bore you with police procedurals. Suffice to say I was discovered. Stripped of her starring role in the *Grand Guignol*, mother had turned to backstabbing to keep her young. This was her *tour de force*. I was a delicious scandal in the streets of Paris for the shortest of times. Dive actress shoots playboy aristocrat! The audience for my beheading was smaller than my mother's had been, but then she had been a star in her time and I knelt at the guillotine barely an ingénue. I should like to say the crowd seemed to disappear then, and that in my last moments I remembered my love as he had been before he fell to cowardice. But that would be one lie too far. No, I drank in the whispers and whoops of the people. I bathed in the blue of the sky above me. I smiled to think of my own severed head and the thrill of horror my death would give the baying crowd. The blade dropped, blinding in the winter sunlight.

Consciousness disengaged from the body.

I died.

Shall I pour you a drink? You look like you could use one. There. Take your time. Yes, if you like, I *am* a poltergeist. It doesn't really work that way, but it's as good a definition as any. Time to go? Oh, no. Do you suppose I have a pressing engagement at – goodness, is that the time? I'll have a drink too. I'll need one, before I tell you the story of my afterlife. Now *that* is a story.

Are you sitting comfortably?

The Wish Dog

Maria Donovan

Before she arrived, I boxed up all the spirits and put them in the attic. I hadn't seen her for nearly fourteen years, until she tracked me down online – and even then we didn't fall into each other's arms: for a while we were just virtual friends.

From things she said I gathered that for her the years had not been kind; when she asked if she could come and stay I didn't say no: I rang her up. It took a minute to tune her voice into my memory. 'So,' she said, 'you still have the dog.'

'Of course.' He has his own account on Twitter. I follow him and he follows me.

'And hasn't he gone grey?'

Back when she knew him, his face was almost completely black; now it is almost completely white.

'I'd like to come and see you,' she said. 'But you know what they say: "let sleeping dogs lie".'

'Never mind the metaphors,' I said. 'Thinking literally: I was looking at him today and – you know when they're young you think it's about getting some peace for yourself? Then one day you see him struggle just to stand up. "Let sleeping dogs lie": it's about giving him some peace now.'

'You should keep him going,' she said. 'Keep him walking.'

'Oh, I look after him; don't you worry.'

'So how about it? I could do with a break.'

I did owe her something, so I said yes. When she texted me with her arrival time, she added, 'I've missed you. Why did we ever fall out?'

As if she didn't know.

I picked her up from the train station; she was wearing a chunky blue hand-knitted cardigan and big boots; her hair was still long with orange streaks but now it was also grey at the roots. When we hugged she held on to me longer than felt comfortable and I kept patting her back until she let go. Then I helped her with her suitcase and her bags. 'You should see me when I go away for the weekend,' I said, loading the car. 'I've always got so much stuff – what with the dog's bed and food and bowls and everything.'

She peered into the back seat. 'Didn't you bring him with you?'

'He was in his bed, snoring. And I had to go shopping – but we can stop again if there's anything you want.'

'Nothing,' she said. 'Unless we need to pick up something to drink?'

'Oh that's okay,' I said. 'I've got some in.'

We set off. 'Anyway,' I said, after some small talk about her trip, 'I thought you'd stopped drinking.'

'I have,' she said. 'But now I'm here …'

I could feel her looking at me. 'Remember that time you

fell off the wagon?' I said, keeping my eyes on the road. 'That's when you brought home the dog.' I could feel my heart picking a hole in my chest.

I had thought about telling her my side of the story, but maybe I would wait until nearer the end of her visit.

She didn't know he was a Wish Dog, that I'd decided I wanted him long before she brought him home, how I'd thought hard about it: what it would mean to walk six miles a day and more, to give him a good and loving home for the rest of his life. I'd been careful in my wishing: I wanted him to be black, medium-sized, thin-coated so he wouldn't shed hairs, good with children and other animals, a go-anywhere kind of dog. I wanted a boy but I did not want him to have a bad smell.

The night she fell off the wagon was near Christmas. She'd been on it a month so it was quite a hard fall. She came home late and tapped on the door of my room. This was new. Usually she just turned the music up loud and played it till three in the morning, while she searched the cupboards for alcohol and soaked up every last drop in the house. I had given up trying to help her. 'You're going to be so angry,' she slurred.

I went with her to her room and as soon as I saw this little black dog with his head bowed, I had to stop myself saying, 'That's him!'

He'd been living under a bush and eating fallen burger buns and chips from the gutter, until two young girls found him and took him to the pub, where people treated him to crisps and cold sausages. My friend was the last to leave and the barmaid persuaded her to take him home. 'The dog warden's coming tomorrow,' said my friend. 'But he can sleep on my bed tonight.' The barmaid told me later, she thought if my friend had to care for another living creature, she might take better care of herself.

'Do you want to keep him?' I said. 'Because if you're not sure, it would be kinder to make him comfortable down in the kitchen.'

I was so calm about it that she agreed. The next day, I got up and took him for a walk and gave him breakfast. At mid-morning the dog warden came and I asked him to wait while I woke her up. She came down, bleary and bedraggled. He asked if she would like to keep the dog and she said, 'No. No, I like him but – I don't think I can look after him.'

Slowly, I said, 'Then, I think, I would like to try.'

She stared at me with bloodshot eyes. 'The landlord won't like it,' she said.

'He'll be OK.' I was a good tenant. He'd known me a long time. I decorated the house. I kept it tidy. I made sure the bills were paid.

The dog warden said, 'As long as you keep him till after Christmas.' Before Christmas is their busiest time, he said, when last year's puppies are abandoned.

'I will,' I said.

'A dog's not just for Christmas,' she said.

'This one might be,' I countered, but I knew that I would keep him. She started to hate me then: I accepted that. But she seemed to hate the dog too. Mostly she ignored him. Sometimes she laughed because it hadn't all been easy – not at first. He was so used to being a stray he'd run off after anything: bicycles, horses, other dogs, children, any kind of food. But he always came back. And when I bent down to stroke him for the first time, and sniffed the top of his head, he smelled so sweet and clean, just like my old teddy bear.

'You do live out in the wilds,' she said.

'Well,' I said. 'I did warn you.'

As we climbed higher we entered the clouds. When we got to the house, tall and detached, rising out of the mist, she said, 'So you live here all on your own? No neighbours?'

I smiled. 'Half a mile away. And I have the dog of course. I'd probably like to live in a town again but this will do us until he dies. Unless you want to buy it?'

She snorted and said nothing. We parked at the side and went in at the front gate, past the For Sale sign lying flat on its back in the garden. 'The wind blew it down,' I said. 'No point sticking it up again unless there's a viewing.' I unlocked the door. 'It's great for now: I only have to open the back door and he's got the run of the fields all to himself.'

'A dog is a social animal,' she said, struggling in with her bags. 'Isn't it a bit cruel to keep him here with no friends?'

For all her talk, she took no notice of him when he came to greet her. She just dumped her things in a pile in the hallway and said, 'Go on then, you might as well give me the tour. I know you're dying to.'

'You don't want a cup of tea?'

'No no,' she said. 'Lead on.' Her eyes were everywhere: we did upstairs first – she picked a bedroom and I showed her where the dog slept at night so she wouldn't trip over him if she went to the bathroom – then down to the kitchen, the sitting-room and the conservatory. The dog followed us trying to sniff her trousers, getting under our feet each time we turned around. We entered the study last: full circle back to the front hall. I wanted her to admire my wall of books, my desk, my woodburner, my cosy sofa, my freestanding floor lamp, but she stopped dead on the threshold and gasped. She wouldn't follow us in. Instead, she shuddered and put up her hands like a mime artist finding a wall. 'Oh! I can't go in there,' she said. 'I can feel a terrible chill – as if there's a … a presence. I'm very sensitive to these things.'

I, who had already crossed over, gave her a look. 'Or you might be sensitive to the almighty draught coming through the letterbox.'

She folded her arms. 'You don't believe in ghosts?'

'Look,' I said, firmly. 'This house is a hundred years old. Someone will have died here. So let's just say that if there are any ghosts they must be happy.'

Still she wouldn't come in: too stubborn to admit that a current of cold air could just be a current of cold air. 'Whatever,' she said, turning away. 'I need a drink.'

Clouds pressed against the windows. Sparrows and blue tits chased each other on and off the bird feeders hanging from a gnarly old willow. We sat in the conservatory sipping beer while the dog went to fetch her a toy. Again she looked around as if she'd come to value the furniture.

I thought if I had a drink too then she might stop when I did. All I had downstairs was beer and wine. I had to hope she wouldn't sniff out the hard stuff in the attic. She could hardly let down the ladder in the night and if she did, well, I might just push it up again and leave her there. 'Cheers,' I said and we clinked bottles. 'It's a shame it's foggy,' I said. 'We have a great view of the sea from here, and the mountains, on a clear day.' I swept my arm to indicate the panorama we were missing.

'Oh, I'm sure,' she said.

The dog, who had come back with a ball in his mouth, followed my arm and went on looking at something neither of us could see. Lately I've come upon him staring at his own shadow on the wall. Sometimes, I have to turn him round and give him a little push to make him go in the right direction. She didn't want to talk about the dog; she wanted to ask how much the house was worth, what did I plan to do next.

The dog dropped the ball at her feet. 'He's trying to impress you,' I said. 'Oh, it's gone under the sofa.' She reached down and pulled the ball out covered in fluff. I decided to show no embarrassment. 'Sorry,' I said. 'I forgot to dyson under the furniture.'

'At least you have a Dyson,' she said. 'At least you have furniture.'

She held the ball between finger and thumb and looked

at it before offering it to me and saying with unreasonable sarcasm, 'Don't you want to go out and throw the ball for him?'

'Haven't done that for a while,' I said. 'Too much strain on the joints, stopping suddenly. And now he wouldn't see it anyway.'

'You're saying he can't run after a ball? Surely you can get him to do anything you like?'

Her laugh was hollow and unpleasant; but I had decided to ignore any bad behaviour.

'I wouldn't make him play fetch just to show that he'll do what I want.'

She looked out of the window. The silence went on and I didn't fill it with nervous talk. Show no weakness, that's what I thought: she's up to something. 'Funny,' she said at last. 'I expect you know that a fetch is a kind of ghost: the ghost of something still living.' She turned to me and leaned in. I didn't let myself be her mirror. 'I had a friend once,' she said, 'and when she was ill she felt something looming over her, running up behind her. She saw herself running past. Not long after that, she died.'

This, I thought, is going to be a long weekend. She used to be just a mindless drunk: now she is pompous, solemn and mean. 'Maybe that's why the dog barks at his own reflection in the glass sometimes,' I said.

She stuck out her jaw and said nothing, squinting off into the mist, mouth turned down.

She didn't want to come for a walk. When I fed him, she stood over me. 'Do you know what you're doing?' she said.

'I think I know how to take care of my own dog!'

She just looked at me. I thought, it's all right for her: she can leave whenever she likes; I have given her the bus timetable; there are taxis. But I can't go.

We went out the next day and didn't take the dog. She seemed relieved. 'Too hot for him in the car,' I said. She wanted to go to the pub and was impatient with me for needing to get home again. I told her: 'The boy will be bursting.'

I walked him round the fields without her and then we settled in for the evening. The day had been clear and as the red disk of the sun slid under the sea, she asked me, the words slopping out of her mouth. 'Why did you want me to come here?'

I smiled and asked her, 'Why did you want to come?'

'Maybe I just wanted to see the dog again. It's been… weird and, if I'm honest, a bit creepy.'

'Oh!' I said. 'I'm so sorry.'

'Now you're offended.'

'Not at all. I don't like to bear grudges.'

'Ah, so it's still about that.'

'About what?'

'Oh you know. You know. The disappearing dog? Come on!'

I said nothing.

'You know,' she said, 'at first I thought you just wanted to show off. This place. Lady of the Bloody Manor. But now – you just want to get back at me, don't you?'

'For what? The Worst Weekend of My Life? You think I'm still angry about that?'

'What else?' she said.

I was silent, tenderly probing my own feelings. I could see this annoyed her more than ever.

'It was an incident,' I said. 'We should never have allowed it to spoil our friendship.' I was being careful because we had at least one more night to spend under the same roof. 'In a funny way,' I said, 'I realise now, it was as much my fault as yours.'

One morning, a few months after his arrival, the dog and I had a falling out. I was in a hurry to get off to work and he was more interested in the neighbours' bins than in coming back to me. I had to go and grab his collar, put him on the lead and march him home. When I left that day I remember we looked at each other with very little liking. I thought, maybe I had made a mistake. Maybe I didn't want this dog after all. Still, I hurried back in my lunch hour to let him out.

When I got home, he was gone.

The back door was locked. I looked in every room, under the beds and even in the cupboards. Nothing. She was out too, so I thought, maybe she's taken him. I tried not to get angry.

The neighbours from across the street saw me on the pavement looking up and down. They told me they'd seen him hanging around at the front of the house and then he chased a bicycle down the road, barking; the cyclist tried to kick him and nearly fell off; they didn't see what happened to the dog.

I ran down the street to where the houses ended and the lane began, past the allotments to the bridge, then back through the fields and home, hoping to find him waiting for me.

She was in the house.

'Is he with you?' I gasped. 'Have you seen him?'

She looked furtive. She told me she had opened the back door and he had jumped over into the neighbours' yard. 'Their gate was open,' she said, 'so he got out.'

'So he was in the alley. Why didn't you just get him back?'

She shrugged. 'I was late. I had to go.'

I wanted to shake her. 'How could you?' I said. 'That poor little dog.'

I phoned the dog warden in case he had been found. I looked for him in all our favourite haunts and then rushed home in case he had returned. What if he came back and couldn't get in? What if he thought I didn't care? I put up notices in corner shops and gave dog walkers my number. I left the door open at night and went outside and stood in the quiet dark street, looking at the stars and wishing with all my heart for him to come back. I could not settle or think of anything else.

Late on Sunday afternoon I was once again outside the front door, wondering how I could go to work on Monday, when far away in the distance I saw a black dot. It grew bigger and bigger, hurrying down the middle of the street, sprouting ears and legs. There he was, coming straight towards me, head down as if he thought he was in trouble. I bent down and he came straight in and tucked his head under my arm. 'You're back,' I cried. 'You're back!' He was filthy and exhausted. I fed him and gave him a bath and he slept until the following day. When I went to work I made sure he was safe in my room. He and I did not fall out again. We always kept an eye on each other.

The same could not be said for me and my friend. I hardly spoke to her after that. At no point did I tell her that I had wished for the dog and then changed my mind: no wonder he had disappeared. When he returned, I had my second chance. I did not doubt my luck again.

When, all these years later, she found me online, I thought: perhaps I'm meant to tell her now, because I can't keep him for much longer; the years will take him from me; I will have to let him go.

I thought about giving her the full story on the last night of her visit but – she was drunk again. She hadn't changed. And they do say that if you work magic, you should never speak of it. She wouldn't understand and even after all this time I knew that something could be lost.

She narrowed her eyes and pointed a finger and said, 'So – where do you think he is now?'

'By the back door. I'll let him out and then I'm off to bed.'

When she got up and stood behind me and I locked eyes with her reflection, I felt I had to quickly shut the door on him and turn the key, in case she tried to push me out and leave me on the wrong side. I could feel her jealousy: she would like to find a way to take possession of everything we had. At last, she turned and walked into the kitchen and I heard the ting of the pedal bin lid hitting the dresser, so it was safe to open the door and let him back in. As I dried his paws, I thought, what is she throwing away now?

The next day I took her to her train. On the platform she surprised me by hugging me again. Then she held me at arm's length and looked into my eyes and said, 'All weirdness aside – I'm worried about you.'

When I got home I called to my boy. Nothing. For a moment that horrible empty feeling again. She would never know what it was to feel that loss. Then I heard him get up out of his bed. There he was at the top of the stairs, looking down, dark eyes in a white face, tail faintly wagging.

Broad Beach

Eileen Dewhurst

The runner arrives with the sunrise. Two minutes later each morning. Yesterday it was 7.20. Today it will be 7.22. Sure enough, as 7.22 glows green on the clock beside the bed there it is, the figure, moving along the edge of the sea. The tide is a long way out this morning so there is a lot of beach between them. Andrew fiddles with the binoculars but he can't quite get the focus and when the phone rings his hand jerks and he loses the figure completely.

'Hello love.' It's Mari, his wife. 'Were you asleep?'

'No. Not really.'

'Another bad night?'

'Pretty much the same as usual.' He doesn't want to worry her. She wouldn't like to hear about the sweating and the dreams. She'd think it was something to do with the medication and make him go back to the GP.

'Oh, good. I'm just off to work now, but I'm just reminding you that Mrs Morris is coming this morning. You haven't forgotten have you?'

He had forgotten. It takes a few moments for the name to register.

'She'll be there just after nine. She seemed nice on the

phone. You take it easy now. And don't overdo the walking will you?'

'I won't. ' He looks down at the binoculars hanging from their strap at his wrist. He's missed the runner. He'll have to wait till tomorrow morning now.

'See you Friday then. I'll do a shop on the way. Let me know if you think of anything you want bringing.'

'I will.'

'Ok. See you soon then. Love you.'

'Love you too.'

Back at the window he looks down to the far end of the bay where there's a parking place with picnic tables and a stream that fizzles out into the pebbles. In summer it's packed with tourists. Not now, not in November. No one comes here much this time of year. Just the runner moving along the line of the tide, making him think of some animal, a race horse or a big cat, loping with easy grace to where the bulk of the headland marks the far side of the bay. Watching the runner is the high spot of the day.

Mrs Morris is a short, wiry woman with a grey glint in her eyes that unnerves him. She knows the story. How he 'died' in A & E, was clinically dead for, oh, minutes, but how they managed to get him back. How she knows, he's not quite sure. He puts it down to the mysterious osmosis of information that goes on in small villages. Or it might just be Facebook. She makes them the kind of milky coffee that once he would have found disgusting and sits him down in an easy chair that, like the rest of the house, has seen better days.

'You're lucky to get this place,' she informs him, 'It's booked up all summer and most of autumn usually. Being so close to the sea. That's what the visitors want. Sea views.' She eyes his collection of inhalers lined up on the kitchen table. 'Good for you too. Sea air.' Among her many nephews, she tells him, she has two who suffer badly from asthma. 'They'll grow out of it.' She says with confidence. 'People usually do.' She doesn't actually say, 'Why haven't you?' But he somehow feels himself accused.

Mrs Morris doesn't only have nephews. She has aunts too.

'It must have been quite a thing,' she says, pausing while opening the cupboard under the sink, 'I had an aunt who had one. You know, what happened to you. There was light, she said, and a tunnel.' She holds the pose, eyes glazing, imagining, he supposes, the tunnel.

'Really?' He sighs. Now he has a choice. Embellishment or truth. That she requires embellishment is obvious from the increased level of glitter in the grey eyes. *Reassure me. There are tunnels. There is light. Tell me what I want to hear.*

'Can't say I had that sort of experience,' he says. She selects a bottle from the cupboard, inspects the label, gives it a little shake, as if it is now of more interest to her than him.

'But I did hear a voice.'

'A voice?' Now he has her full attention.

When he was a child, his mother who was Scottish called him Ondrew. It's just the way Andrew came out. Wee Ondrew, that was him. He tells Mrs Morris about his Scottish mother and the way she had of standing on the top step and yelling 'Wee Ondrew' down the street at the top of her voice. Mrs Morris nods in a way that indicates she approves of the fact that he had a Scottish mother if nothing else.

'It was as if,' he says, sitting up slightly, 'I was on my way somewhere and I had to stop. I could hear my mother calling me back.'

'Ah ha!' Mrs Morris glitters.

What had happened was that one of the nurses had the same sort of accent as his mother. She kept on saying things like, come on Ondrew, you can do it Ondrew, in an encouraging way. But then Mrs Morris frowns.

'You'd think she'd be telling you to go back though wouldn't you? Go back! Not yet! Something like that?'

Andrew shrugs and leans back into the chair. There you are; the truth is never quite what's required. But Mrs Morris isn't finished with him yet. She tidies the room, goes upstairs to make his bed, comes down, declares it a war zone, and makes another cup of coffee. Then she tells him about the dog.

'It was a nice dog,' she says, 'but it bit the postman and that was that. In those days it was gas, not injections like they have now.' She tells him her aunt, a different aunt, not the one who came back from the dead, left it at the vets and then, overtaken by grief and remorse because it was a good dog really, ran back and made the vet rescue it from the sealed kennel. She dragged it back home, half stupefied, where it lived for many years, a gentle and placid thing snoring on the hearth. Lucky, she said, to be alive.

Yes indeed. Andrew agrees. Lucky to be alive.

At 7.24 the following morning, Andrew is back at the window. The bed behind him resembles a war zone again thanks to the dreams. He takes the binoculars out of their case. Looks at them, passes them from hand to hand. They are solid. They are black. They can be touched, weighed. They don't smell of anything much but they are real. They allow him to see way out to the far end of the beach. The tide is further in today. He can see all this. This is real. Nonetheless, he shuffles from foot to foot and glances over his shoulder to the bed where not five minutes ago, in the fog of waking, he had been convinced that a half-doped dog had been asleep, curled up against his right leg, breathing deeply and sonorously as dogs do. He could have sworn he'd put out his hand and stroked the top of a soft and velvety head. It was real. There was warmth; he'd felt it. He knows for sure he had an intense and urgent feeling he should be taking this dog for a walk.

From the window, apart from a couple of seagulls circling for pickings, he can see no other movement with or without the binoculars. According to the laws of nature, the sun must be rising, but it's doing so in private somewhere behind a bank of low, thick cloud. The incoming tide has submerged the broad sweep of sand and is further in this morning. It's lapping at the scattered boulders and rocky outcrops, replenishing the rock pools, washing out the dead things. Maybe the runner has stayed at home. That would be sensible. He can see no sign of anyone moving along the shore. Maybe the runner only runs when the tide is out, when it's possible to get round the headland and into the next bay.

Getting to sleep and staying asleep have been a problem for a while. He's never mastered the art of sleeping sitting up, he wakes often with a start, perhaps he's swallowed his tongue, perhaps he has sleep apnoea. He knows he snores from twenty years of being nudged awake by Mari. Has he always been a nuisance then? It's the dreams that are new. Full on Technicolor dreams, full of sensory intensity, complete with voices, smells, textures. The first one arrived on the night after being discharged from hospital. He'd woken up, or believed he'd woken up, and gone down the stairs holding onto the smooth wooden banister, he could smell the polish, to where his mother was making breakfast in their kitchen. Porridge, with a sprinkle of salt, the Scottish way.

'Come along now Ondrew,' she'd said in her usual brisk way, tying on her pinny. He could hear the kettle boiling away, rattling on the stove; could taste the salt on his lips.

When he woke, the sleep still gumming up his eyes, he'd gone down the stairs amazed that the banister was painted not polished, and peered into the kitchen expecting her to be there. He looked for her. He even opened the back door and called her name.

'Excessive dreaming can sometime happen with a bit of low mood,' the GP says writing out his next prescription. Mari has signed him up with the local GP surgery as a temporary resident. Andrew has casually asked about dreams, just in passing. Low mood? What does that mean?

'Do you think I'm depressed?'

‘Well, lots of people are.’ The waiting room outside is full of old people coughing and babies crying. He’s sorry he mentioned the dreams.

‘It’s not uncommon though, especially after what you’ve been through. Is there anything else bothering you?’

‘No, of course not.’ He has Mari his lovely wife who is coming at the weekend. He has a delightful daughter who has a wonderful husband. They’re both employed and are expecting their first baby. He has an excellent health insurance policy and his pension pot is doing fine. There’s an office desk waiting for him just as soon as he feels himself to be fit and well. What could possibly be wrong?

Back at the house, it’s clear Mrs Morris has been in. She must have been colluding with Mari because the fridge appears to be full of food. The telephone answer machine is flashing.

Hi darling. I might have to be a bit later on Friday. Or it might even have to be Saturday. Something’s come up at work. You know how it is. I’ve asked Mrs Morris to get the shopping in so I won’t have to stop off on the way. How’s it going? Mrs Morris said you’d gone to the GP. Hope they’ve sorted you out OK. Don’t go overdoing it now. Look after yourself. See you soon. Love you.

She sounds as if she’s reading from a script, is in a hurry to be off. There’s a note in her voice he hasn’t heard before.

Once, a long time ago, when he was still Ondrew, he’d run for the school in the cross-country team. He tries to remember what it was like, the heart pound, the rush of blood, his lungs, efficient and full of life. He's brought a vest, shorts and a pair of running shoes with him even though running is against instructions. Walking is the thing. He must build up the distance slowly, being careful to use the inhalers as directed. His walk is scheduled for around two in the afternoon, before the air gets too cold and makes his lungs constrict. At 2 p.m. he walks in his running shoes over the shingle beach at the front of the house, clambers over the rocky outcrops with the rock pools and their hidden residents of crabs and starfish; it's easy to slip on the treacherous green seaweed, but he keeps his balance and continues on to where the tide line is edging slowly back in.

There's a set of footprints about to be obliterated by the incoming tide. A runner? His runner? The prints have clearly been made by running feet; the depth is at the front, where the ball of the foot pushes off. The shoe size is the same as his. He steps into the prints. Lifts off from the right foot, propels himself forward. Run. Don't walk. Run. Come on Ondrew. After a few yards, he feels his ribs like an iron cage. He slows back to a walk. The footprints move on without him towards the headland. He has to stand still, just for a moment. He looks down at his feet, ridiculous he thinks, shod in techno-silver, with bright white flashes. Pegasus. If he had the breath, he would laugh.

The house is the end one of a row of three separated from the beach by a low stone wall. The bedroom he is occupying is at the top corner and has two windows so that it looks both south and west at the same time. Walking back, in slow time, he looks towards it, casually noticing that it could do with a coat of paint and then he stops. Looks more closely. He could swear there's a face at the western-facing window. The face is pressed close up to the glass. He can't tell, it's just a little too far away, but he thinks the face is looking out through binoculars. Mrs Morris of course. She'll have forgotten some errand for Mari and will be wondering where he is.

'You don't have to come you know, not if it's too difficult.'

Mari has phoned again from a hotel somewhere in Yorkshire. She works for a small executive travel company which in spite of the recession is doing well. There are always winners, always losers. She's on the winning side and loving every minute.

'I'm so sorry. I was really looking forward to a lovely quiet weekend with you. Next weekend should be fine. We've got the house for a few weeks yet. You enjoy it. What will you do?'

'I've got some films. And a couple of books. Sleep I suppose. I'll be fine.'

'Well, don't let that food go to waste!'

'I won't.' Andrew puts the receiver back in its holster. It has weight, not much, but some; it has a couple of lights that flash indicating battery life. It's real. Her words, although disembodied are real. He can tell himself this but he somehow doesn't feel it to be true.

When he wakes after his early night, it feels like the

middle of the night. Something has disturbed him. Was it a sound? There's an echo of something that sounds like his name but that can't be because there's no one else here. No, his own breathing probably, his mouth is dry as dust and the side of his tongue is sore, as if he's bitten down on it with one of the sharp canine teeth. Although the luminous clock by the bed shows 4.45 a.m. there's a soft glow on the other side of the curtains. He pulls them apart and there's the beach, lit up in the softest of light shining down from the full moon hanging above the bay. He knows this is beautiful. He knows this is the sort of scene poets write about, lovers dream about. Mari would love this. Once she would have slid her arm around his waist and leaned her head on his shoulder. He stares out at it unmoved. It's not that it isn't beautiful. It's not that he wishes there was someone here to share it with him. It is all just somehow unimportant. None of this has anything to do with him.

And then, from the eastern side of the beach, the runner appears. Why not? The light is almost as bright as on a normal November day and the tide is way, way out, leaving the way to the bay clear and easy. He presses his face up against the window. Such movement, the stretch of legs, the upright body, he can imagine, almost feel the wind pushing at his face, rushing into nostrils, down into the lungs, breathing, in and out, feet light on wet sand, almost flying, so alive. He reaches for the binoculars, searches quickly along the shingle, the rocks with their pools and out onto the wet stretch of sand and manages to fix on the runner. But only because the runner has stopped, is stationary, is standing just ahead of where low foamy waves are breaking, and is looking back at him. Startled, Andrew lowers the binoculars. When he lifts them again, the runner has gone.

It's clear now, what it is he needs to do. Oblivious of the sharp cold air, Andrew sheds his pyjamas. He puts on the clothes he has brought for running, a vest and shorts. He ties up the laces of his running shoes. Outside the wind is bitter. He feels its bite immediately and gasps, amazed that it's possible to be this cold. He starts to run. He'll warm up soon. He can see where the moon is making a path of light around the headland. He catches up with the footprints and this time he can keep up. He is so full of running he feels his heart will burst.

Making Ghosts

Sue Moules

'Do you believe in ghosts Mair?' Sarah asks me, as we sew the sheets into ghost costumes. I usually give yes or no answers, but for this I have to prevaricate.

'Maybe,' I say.

I didn't like to say that I'd never seen a ghost, especially as Sarah believes in the supernatural. The village school is old, and was supposed to be full of ghosts. Full of damp and dust more like, but we are lucky still to have the village school.

Once there had been three shops and a post office. Now the shop is also the post office, and the general store. There had been Dilly's Wool Shop and the Sweet Shop, but both had closed due to lack of custom. Everyone went to the superstore in town or shopped online, which meant that the quiet village became busy with supermarket delivery vans. I'm old enough to remember when the shop had a delivery boy on a bike with a basket full of boxed orders.

"I think the old dead folk are the ghosts in this village." Sarah says. 'Mrs Connolly's out pruning her roses in her dressing gown, and Cyril the blacksmith is outside the pub, which is now a private house, but I can see him there. Both of them died when I was a child.'

‘Yes,’ I say. ‘I imagine seeing several of them as I walk around, but I always think it’s because those old black and white photos are in the village hall. Those people have never left. These living children, who are enjoying being ghosts, will move away, but something of them will remain.’

‘I hope so,’ Sarah says. It seems a shame that villages just get forgotten, they become assimilated into the town’s catchment area and become districts. ‘So, do you think these “Save our School” ghosts will frighten the councillors?‘

‘No,’ I say, ‘but they will be good for publicity and the photographs in the *Gazette* will help make others more aware of our campaign.’

The evening was drawing in. I got up to pull the curtains. I saw a face at the window. I heard myself scream.

‘There’s someone there…’ I said. We went outside into the dusk with a torch and the dog. There was no one there, but the dog’s fur bristled, and he growled as he passed the window.

‘It’s your imagination, Mair,’ said my husband, ‘and all those ghost costumes you’ve been sewing. Come on now, we’ll take the dog for a walk. That will reassure you there’s nothing there but stars.’

He was right, just stars and the quiet of the village graveyard, where I wouldn’t walk at night because there’s something about a graveyard at night that needs to be left to its own.

*

The ghost costumes didn't save the school. It's been sold and is now a private home. Incomers bought it; too expensive for locals. The eight village children are now bussed to school in town. Their faces in the minibus windows are like ghosts. Their names echo the ones on the gravestones : Tomos Davies, Elwyn Jones, Siôn Thomas, Rhodri Williams, Elin Thomas, Siân Hughes, Betsan Davies, Megan ap Rhys.

A Matter Of Light

Elizabeth Baines

1816

May 1st
Never having been a man much given to journal-making but spending my life in the practical matters of trade, I am minded now, in my seventy-sixth year and possessing greater leisure (my youngest son having taken on the greater burden of our business), to write of certain curious phenomena of light which I have recently witnessed within the walls of my home. To my knowledge no other member of my household has likewise made such sightings, for which I must be grateful, since there is a strangeness about them that could unsettle those of weak or uneducated mind.

All of my acquaintance, here and abroad, will vouch for me as a rational man, and I mean to set down in the spirit of scientific observation the particulars of these incidents, which have indeed occurred in broad daylight, and in a house but twenty-five years built – to my own commission and personal specification – and thus no likely repository for hauntings by previous deceased incumbents, even should one hold with the desire or ability of unquiet spirits to wander into our physical domain.

My house, standing as it does on an open hill just beyond the sweep of the town, faces not to the past but to the future, with clean lines and spacious rooms looking out to the rear down a hill towards the river and the misty hills beyond, and equipped with the latest devices for household convenience. My study is a room of calm proportions and, being on the ground floor, lit by one of the tallest windows, a place conducive to clarity of thought, contemplative study and the judicious conduct of business transactions. It is in this room that, two days ago, the first of the events to which I refer occurred.

It was mid-morning. I was alone and at my desk, reading an account by the Reverend Smythe of an attempt to transfer mulberry trees to warmer climes. The sun made a wide beam across the beige carpet in the centre of the room. I stood from my desk beside the window and crossed to the bookcase on the left-hand wall. As I did so, a movement to the right caught my eye. I thought that my servant had entered unnoticed, but in the next moment I knew I remained quite alone. I considered that my movement across the room had created an answering shadow, until I saw that my shade was falling away from me in the opposite direction, across the beige carpet and onto the wall on the left.

In truth, it was at the time a little thing, for my mind was much on the mulberry tree and its transplantation, and my curiosity was mild as I stepped back to the window and looked out to see what reflection or refraction had thrown perhaps the shadow of a bird against the usual trajectory. Looking out I saw nothing but the empty road and the rise beyond nodding with cowslips, and my thoughts returned to my studies.

I should have thought no more of it, had not something further occurred yesterday afternoon.

It is true that, since my wife is a fastidious keeper of this house, in spite of our large windows we are often much shrouded in shadow, the curtains pulled to protect the furnishings from bleaching by the sun. The lower staircase, however, is ever an airy sweep of light, its pale stone and open ironwork balustrade lit by a long window that looks out to the westerly hills. Yesterday afternoon I was mounting the first flight when I noticed on the wall beside the window the shadow of a man, head and shoulders sans periwig, merging below into a less distinct column. I looked around me quickly, expecting to see someone behind down the stairs or up on the landing. No one was there, but it struck me that it should have been strange even had they been so, for light comes only from the uncurtained window, thus casting shadows in the opposite direction, and no mirror is hung on any of the walls or on the landing above or in the hall down below to send back any rays. When I looked back the shadow had gone, and I will confess that I did then suffer a moment's unease, and the sense of encountering a Being, and the hairs on my neck did prick, before I mastered such thoughts that belong to base and irrational lore.

It is a most curious phenomenon which I cannot account for by my own previous studies of refraction, and which has much excited my scientific curiosity. I have this day sent to

London for a copy of Thomas Young's paper to the Royal Society concerning the properties of light.

May 6th

I have perused Mr Young's experiments, which proved that light is capable of being bent (and is thus made of waves rather than corpuscles as had been previously held), including his double-slit experiment in which two beams of light interfering with each other did indeed create stripes of shadow. But this yet does not explain how any shadow so created should appear on my wall quite against any beams of light entering my stairway.

I shall watch for further instances and record them carefully. I have all my life endeavoured to avoid the sin of pride, disliking ostentation in matters of both material wealth (I have ensured that my home, though large, is simply furnished) and intellect, yet I cannot but feel that to make a discovery that may contribute to the greater field of scientific knowledge would be the crowning glory of an assiduous and careful life.

I have not shared with my wife this hope, nor anything of the circumstance. She is stout of heart but she has suffered with her health since we settled in this rheumy part of the world; moreover, she has never put behind her the old superstitions, and would conclude that we have been invaded by ghosts.

May 8th

I have once more witnessed the shadow on the stairs. All

was as before apart from the time of day and the fact that on this occasion I watched the shape disappear, which occurred not instantly, as with a sudden change of light or movement away of an object, but gradually, the object fading slowly before my eyes until no smudge of it remained. This pleases me, confirming perhaps some new character of light as yet unobserved and requiring investigation, light bending perhaps without the aid of mirrors from another vicinity altogether, and explaining those distortions which throughout history have been taken to be ghosts.

May 10th

No further occurrence of the light/shadow phenomenon, but I have been much taken up with other matters, not only my ship coming to harbour and involving me and my son with merchants, but another mystery in my household, one involving sound.

I was in the drawing room alone, waiting for my wife to join me, when I heard someone whisper, it seemed from over near the door. I peered but was blinded by the beam of sun coming through the half-drawn curtains, and could make out nothing in the gloom beyond. The whisper came again, a rustle that resolved itself into what seemed to me a human voice, though I could not make out the words. 'Who is there?' I asked, stepping into the gloom. My eyes accustomed themselves, and I saw that there was no one there. My eye alighted on the horn of the speaking tube, my house being most usefully equipped with an ingenious system, still unknown to many. A series of tubes connects the kitchen to the upper rooms, the servants being summoned by blowing through a horn at the upper end and activating a whistle at the lower, so saving much running about of servants, and the purse of the master who may thus employ fewer. I deduced that this was whence the sound had come, the whistle at the lower end having become detached and sound from the kitchen allowed to travel upwards. I tried it, my wife entering the room just then. The whistle sounded at the other end, and we thought that it must have been quickly replaced, yet when the maid appeared and my wife called her to account she averred that the whistle had been in place all along, and her manner was so sincerely upset that I do not know if the problem is a mechanical one needing my attention or a servant problem for my wife.

May 15th

I continue to hear whispering sounds. I now hear them along the landings, and I do not know how any sound from the speaking tubes could reach there. I have ventured to risk frightening my wife by asking her if she hears anything too, but she says she does not.

And always I hear them when I am alone.

I will confess that I am a little ruffled. Today as I was about to enter the drawing room, the sound came from along the corridor towards the back of the house, a hoarse sibilance seeming to snake towards me, and just as it stopped there was another sound like the scrape of a foot, as if someone were ducking out of sight. I turned quickly, my blood thumping, but the long space was quite empty, all the doors firmly shut.

I fear that I am of a sudden pushed by old age from my rational character. All of my life have I conducted myself with equanimity and reason. No vicissitude has ever knocked me from my senses – no storm at sea, no grief, not the deaths of two of my beloved children, nor the waywardness of my elder sons. That those sons should reject my very principles of rationality and align themselves with poets and dreamers and, like their mother, be happy to submit to the promptings of feeling and of imagined spirits, was indeed to me a matter of both puzzlement and chagrin. It is hard for a man who believes in a life of rigour – hard work, early rising, regular and healthy meals and a daily plunge in a cold bath – to countenance his sons lounging in their opium dens, wigless in the way that is now the fashion, their hair awry. Yet I reasoned that no good comes of quarrelling with one's children, and I took pains to accommodate them, so far even as to extend hospitality to their poet friends.

I think it may be said that I dealt fairly with my children, and with all whom I have encountered, which is a steadying thought to have in one's closing years.

No further sign of the light/shadow business to date.

May 17th

My discomposure continues.

A most odd happening when my wife and I were alone

at dinner today. We enjoy the benefit of that modern invention, the dumb waiter, whereby food may be sent straight up to us from the kitchen without the need of human carrying. We are attacking our pudding today when a most prodigious sound of young girls giggling seems to burst from the shaft, and the cry, 'Loök!' in a strange accent, as if some new maid, brought from other parts, were hollering up the hole. 'God's truth,' cries I to my wife, most annoyed that this contraption, designed not only to bring the food to us piping hot, but also to afford us a privacy hitherto unattainable in a house with servants, should allow such disruption of our peace. My wife looks at me blankly. Says I, 'Do you countenance such indiscretion by servants?' She wants to know of what indiscretion I speak. She has heard no giggling and no sound whatever.

Perhaps my wife is going deaf, I think, and believe that she feared so too.

Yet tonight she tells me that no new maids have been employed, and that the cook when spoken to maintained that there were none in the kitchen at the time when we ate our pudding, one having been sent to the underground store for butter, the other outside for water.

My wife tells me, laughing: 'You have frightened the cook. She is afraid we are haunted.'

I laughed too, though I cannot claim that I felt at ease. My wife, whose fear of the supernatural has hitherto amused me, patted my arm in a matter-of-fact way and went to her withdrawing room.

I stepped out on to the landing. And then I thought I

heard it again, fainter now, somewhere in the upper spaces of the house where no servants should be at that time, a voice calling, the words indistinguishable, and then a roiling of giggles, a trickling, bubbling sound.

Rain on the roof perhaps, I thought, that's all, but could not deny the broad sheet of sun lying on the pink stone of the stairs.

May 20th

I fear that I am now truly losing my reason.

Investigation of the system for channelling water from the roof to the tank on the lowest level has yielded no lack or fault likely to cause these unaccustomed sounds, which I have since heard yet again. My personal examination of the dumb waiter found no mechanism worn and no piece of crockery overlooked and rattling. Unless I am to succumb to a belief that ghosts walk this house, I must conclude that my eyes and ears have been deceiving me all along, and that this must extend to the shadows as well as sounds.

Today I looked up from my desk and thought I saw a man standing across the room. In an instant he was gone, and I knew him for what he was, a moment's vision, a dream, but what lasted in my mind was the gaze he seemed to beam towards me, a gaze of accusation.

Yet, just as I do not hold that any ghost has the capacity to rise up to reproach me, neither do I think that my conscience should do so. In all my dealings I have treated others with consideration. I did not disown my sons when they quarrelled with my philosophy; I even smuggled to safety one of their group in trouble for his radical activities. I made pains to understand and assuage my wife's sad longings, arranging her frequent journeys to the land of her birth. Our close servants have been treated as family, my man, a manumitted slave, enjoying many of the freedoms of any young English gentleman.

I should rather submit to the notion that we are haunted than to believe I am so far thrust from my reason as to imagine these presences. Yet what ghost would appear as these do, away from the traditional time of night and in the blare of the sun which flings itself in a gold river down our stairway turning to diamonds the fine sugar on the table, substance of my trade?

May 21st

Not long since, this very evening, I suffered a most distressing vision. I had repaired to our bedroom to change for dinner. The maid had failed to pull the curtains and sun was filling the room, light glancing off the washstand and the pure white dimity bed frills, dazzling my eyes. I went to the window to look down the valley, and experienced an alarming sensation. The view was quite changed: pale slabs of colour blocked the view of the river, as if films had formed before my eyes. I turned in. I felt blinded and giddy.

I heard voices I did not recognise on the landing.

I staggered rather than stepped into the dressing room and, though later I would find the room restored to its customary state, in that moment it appeared to me quite bare, bulging with sun and the curtains and furnishings all gone.

Yet there in this dream, writ large on a plaque on the wall, were my very own words, my instructions to the managers of my plantations that my slaves should be treated with humanity, that I would not suffer any human being committed by providence to my care to be treated with severity.

It is my eternal sadness that my abolitionist elder sons should have lumped me with those cruel plantation owners who beat their slaves to death. It was nothing to my sons in their blinkered idealism that when I inherited my first plantation I freed the ill and starving slaves; they preferred to point to the financial saving which this admittedly made, along with the cheapness and investment of the child slaves I replaced them with, and to the economic wisdom rather than the philanthropy of providing my slaves with medical care and clothes and land on which to grow crops of their own. But humanity is surely not diminished by going hand in hand with good economic sense. And humanity must be tempered with justice, and the system maintained if our trade and the prosperity of our land is to continue. If I told my managers not to whip my slaves within hearing of abolitionist visitors, then it were for the sake of harmony rather than the shame my sons thought I should feel.

May 22nd

I see apparitions everywhere. They people the stairs and the landings and hover at the entrance to rooms, and are such as I never could imagine, in outlandish garb in colours of such luminosity that, though I have lived in the brightness of the West Indies, I did not know could exist. They gaze, they peer, at my furnishings and contraptions. They must be ghosts after all, rather than my own projections, for they are alien, and, though I cannot touch them, concrete-seeming, and I do not know what connection they could have with the pictures of black and broken skin now leaking through my mind…

I, King

Melanie Fritz

There's odd. You think you know where you are – lived all your life by here after all, Merthyr born and bred! – and next thing you know is you don't really know.

Rhian's taking her pugs, Mollie and Batman, for a walk. As usual. She scans her surroundings. There's no knowing where the two've run off to in this vaguely familiar, strangely unfamiliar, place.

Rhian walks in a park that hasn't seen a gardener for decades. She walks along a line of mighty oaks towards a mansion, flaming golden in the evening sun. Above the doorbell, the faded name plate reads *I, King*. The door's ajar but no one's in.

You shouldn't walk into kings' castles, or strangers' houses for that matter, but Rhian can't resist the chance to harvest an odd story to tell, and this is truly odd. She wanders through rooms blessed with light. Walls, floors, wardrobes, drawers, tables, chairs and papers, everything's old and faded and covered in a thin layer of mould. Not dust; not cobwebs; mould. Rhian's checked. There's bouquets of rotting roses in cracked vases and dirty curtains in shreds, stirring gently in the breeze.

Rhian admires the stale beauty of this place. She half

expects to find a royal mummy sitting in a mouldy armchair; or a throne perhaps, like they got loads round here. There's really no one in, however, not even the king's secretary. In the end, Rhian shrugs and leaves. Back outside the air's fresh and clear. She coughs mould out of her system while she walks back down the line of oaks. Mollie and Batman come running towards her yelping with joy and Rhian feels silly. She knows exactly where she is.

For once, she isn't too keen on telling a story and keeps the episode to herself. She ought to tell someone, really, to cough it out of her system – because her inner eye wanders back there time and time again. It was old; it was mouldy; it was creepy; but of an odd beauty too. Who could she share this with? Who'd care?

'Summin' botherin' yew love?' her boyfriend Jamie asks her that night.

'Nah… I'm fine,' she replies. 'Don' know where I've left my 'ead today, be 'onness…'

'I'll fetch it right back love,' he says, with a smile.

Next day's grey and full of drizzle. Couldn't be more miserable.

'Wha'? Yew takin' the dogs out in tha' weather,' Jamie asks.

'Gerrin' bit fat they are,' Rhian says. 'Need theyer exercise. An' me.'

She's not saying, but she's determined to find out more about that mouldy place today. There's just one problem.

Playing it through in her head as she walks, Rhian's not quite sure where she was yesterday. Where that house is.

She ends up in Cyfarthfa Park, with Mollie and Batman dragging their feet and hanging their heads in the drizzle. Rhian knows there's no mansion round here. Maybe there was once. There might have been. There must have been, given Merthyr's prolific demolition history. At the end of this tree line. Rhian makes a mental note to ask her nan.

She's moithered. She knows she's been inside that house. Not a dream that wasn't. She's been there for real: two streaks of mould she found on her jumper and one on her jeans when she put them in the machine this morning.

Rhian's in a proper mood when she comes back from her walk. She hasn't found that bloody house – her, who knows Merthyr better than the postman!

'Christ, yew been gone f'rages Rhi,' says Jamie when she slams the door. 'Sun shinin' where yew walkin'?'

'I look like it?' she snaps and vanishes into the bog.

In the fortnight that follows, Rhian drags her two pugs on a quest around Merthyr, to likely and unlikely places. The more she tries to find the house, and fails, the angrier she gets. This is getting personal. She has to get back there. How she wants to shout at him, King!

'Aw, I'm well impressed with 'ow fit yew gerrin' ouer Moll an' Bat,' Jamie says when they come back one sombre Sunday afternoon.

With a shy smile, he adds, 'An' yewerself, by the way. Well fit yew are…'

Rhian flinches when he tries to touch her and Jamie pulls a face like he's been stabbed.

'Rhi…' he says softly. 'Wha's … wha's wrong? Wha's goin' on… I…'

Rhian's face, infuriated first, falls. A brick wall comes tumbling down and the clouds of its dust bring tears to her eyes.

'Don' know J… I'm sorry I am love…' she stammers. 'I been so moody lately… Get a pregnancy test tomorrer…'

She takes Jamie's hands and lays his arms round her waist. Gets really close and makes it all good again, right there at the door.

'Well fit yew are, aye…' he whispers. He needs his beauty sleep now.

'Mmh. An' yew J,' Rhian says. She contemplates her boyfriend for a while, all skin and warmth and sweetness. She knows she got a good one there. And she can't understand how she got so obsessed with something so stupid, and let it make him sad.

The air feels fresher, less oppressive somehow, when Rhian takes the dogs out again the next day. She's going nowhere in particular for the first time in epochs and ages, and it feels good. Mollie and Batman sense a change in mood too. They hobble around happily and snap at falling leaves.

It's one of those days. The gale plays merry hell with all that's light and loose. Rhian's hair comes alive like a basket of untamed snakes, she can hardly see where she's going. The sun shoots its fiery light against an anthracite sky. The mansion at the end of the tree line looks pale and somewhat unreal in this light.

Rhian stops dead and stares at the house. She's run up and down all of Merthyr in search for this place, and then she finds it the moment she gives up? Her heart slows and cools. This can't be luck. Someone's pulling strings. She knows she got to turn around and leave, now. Now.

But she doesn't. Her curiosity's piqued. She got to find out what's going on, to tell an odd story after, when it all makes sense.

And the door isn't ajar. It's wide open this time. Him, King, is inviting her in.

Rhian can't help feeling flattered by being so welcome. The moment she passes the threshold she understands much better why she has searched for this place so passionately. Longing it was. A longing to be here again, see this again.

Nothing has changed, but Rhian takes in a lot more detail this time. The chairs, the vases, the roses; how beautiful in their decay. Grand old paintings on the walls; faded to nearly all-black and frosted with mould, they might be blind mirrors. How perfectly gothic, how beautiful. Yellow papers strewn on tables, fallen on the carpets and the wooden floors – Rhian wants them to be full of love letters, longing love letters by him, King, to a nameless lady.

Eager to find this the truth Rhian lifts one of the papers, then another, and another. Old warnings are scribbled in cracked blood across the orginal, faded ink.

Leave while you can and never come back!
GO NOW! QUICK!
Hasten out, dear reader, ere the door is shut forever.

Rhian drops the papers in disgust. How dare these people sully his letters and make them utterly illegible!? How is she supposed to get his messages, just because these jealous fuckers want this beautiful place, want him, King, for themselves? Like fuck she'll do as they say! She'll search the whole house from top to bottom for a clue!

When Rhian comes home, Jamie runs to meet her at the door.

'Rhi! Fucksake, I been worried sick 'bout yew!'

'Juss been round Nat's,' she says quietly.

'An' wha' yew two been up to?' Jamie asks. 'Look at yew? Yew into buildin' work now or wha'.'

Rhian gives him a sombre look.

'Bloody kids wha' carn even afford eggs 'ese days? Don' know whar it is 'ey throw at me, but I do wannw wash thar off now.'

She disappears into the shower for a while, then makes a half-hearted attempt to relive last night with Jamie. She's knackered though, and asleep before he is.

Next day, same thing: she can't find it. With the cunning of desperate longing Rhian works out that she can only get to this ghost of a place by *not* wanting to get there.

Why does he, King, make it so hard for her? Is it to test her determination, her devotion? Sweet pain trickles through her at the very thought of it, makes her go wild.

'Aw! Rhi! Tha' was! Fuckin'! Amazin'!' Jamie shouts.

'I wannw feel tha' forever J,' Rhian admits.

'Aye… Me too,' he says. 'Eternal orgasm…wud do…'

Then he's asleep and Rhian gets out of bed. Ten minutes later she's sat at her nan's kitchen table, sipping a strong brew.

'Yew awright then, sweet'eart?' Nana asks. 'Ow's yewer Jamie?'

'E's all right?'

'There's lovely Rhi. Lovely feller, yewer Jamie.'

'Nana, gorrw ass yew summin', 'bout old Merthyr, like. I been out an' about wi' the dogs quite a bit an' I found this place in the park, there's trees, like reely old oak trees, an' I was assin' myself if there ever been, like, a big 'ouse, a proper manshun, in the old days…'

Rhian's voice trails off as her nan starts to think.

'Well, there ewsed to be thar old 'ouse up the Skeepo, wannit? Tha' was demolished in the sixties… Or where to wazzit…'

Nana tries to remember and there's silence in the kitchen. Then suddenly, Nana's face grows hard and she asks, 'Yew seen a 'ouse where there should be none?'

Rhian shakes her head vigorously.

'No, I 'aven' nana. I's juss askin'.'

'Good,' Nana says. 'Tha's juss reminded me o' summin' whar 'appened – 'bout forty years ago?'

'Whar 'appened forty years ago,' Rhian asks.

'Quite positive I am it 'appened in the sev'nties,' Nana says and loses herself a bit trying to figure out the exact year.

'Yeah, but whar 'appened,' Rhian interrupts her.

'Aw, sumwun vanisht, sweet'eart. Wun o' the Jenkins' girls, carn remember 'er name… Been to a grand old 'ouse, she said, an odd place, she said, quite unreal accordin' to 'er. Went there agen an' never came back. An' thar 'ouse she've been on about no wun found. 'Appened before, my own nan said back then.'

'Odd little story, Nana,' Rhian says. She adds a light laugh, finishes her tea, hugs her nan and returns home. Jamie hasn't noticed she was gone.

Nana hasn't really helped Rhian. All she can do, Rhian reckons, is keep wandering without wanting to reach her Caerbannog too much. She spends all her time outside in the shortening days, a slender body, rosy cheeks, fit pugs.

'Yew not cumin' out wi' us *agen,*' her mates ask her.

'No, she isn',' Jamie replies in her stead. 'She not spendin' time wi' me either, so, if she were givin' sumwun 'er attenshun, it be me.'

Rhian doesn't notice his sad smile when he says that.

She's trying so hard not to think about it that her head's gone blank. She's trying so hard not to get anywhere in particular that she isn't really coming back. It all revolves around not revolving around it.

A thin layer of snow has covered Merthyr tonight and made Rhian even more aware of how out of reach a certain mould-frosted mansion is for her. It's just snow. It's not the same.

Mollie and Batman come running towards her all excited when she comes home.

'Where yew been?' Jamie asks her.

'The ewsual, takin' the dogs for a walk,' Rhian replies.

'Forgot summin' 'en, innit,' Jamie says. He's not looking at her.

'Wha' yew mean, J?' Rhian asks.

'Forgot to take the dogs Rhi,' Jamie says.

She got nothing to say to that.

'An' yew wasn' at Nat's thar other night. This been goin' for months now Rhi. I reckon tha's the way it goes, but I do wonder why yew bother cumin' back. Why yew not stayin' with 'im. Cuz I gorrw leave now, 'aven' I. Yew got two places an' I got none.'

She got nothing to say to that either. She just stands at the door till Jamie's left.

''E's King, J,' she says when he's gone. ''E's King. An' 'e's waitin' for me.'

Rhian feels ashamed. She feels so ashamed for keeping him, King, waiting for so long.

Now that Jamie's gone she's relieved. There's no need to go home anymore; she's free to search for him, King, whenever she likes for as long as she likes. And how sweet it is to search for him, King, trying not to search for him. He knows she's looking for him, and she needs to trick him, King, into believing she's not. What a sweet game, what a sweet, sweet pain. What determination. What devotion.

Rhian's been walking for the last forty-three hours. She

knows Merthyr better than the postman, aye. She's past the need for sleep, and at about eleven that night, she's past herself too. She doesn't remember herself or Merthyr or mouldy mansions or him, King. She doesn't remember she's walking, she just walks, and she walks into a park, and along a line of trees, and towards a wide open door.

As soon as she's inside Rhian's all there again. She's so overjoyed she throbs and wails. She's made it back! She got it right! She does need to be oblivious of how to get here! Otherwise it doesn't work! And now, she's found a way of achieving this oblivion! She'll be able to return whenever she wants!

Rhian cries and cries. She wanders through the rooms crying, stroking the mouldy furniture, the paintings and walls, like the soft fur of a beloved pet. Rhian lifts a rose out of her vase and smells at it, the rotting petals touching her nose, lips, tongue and chin. Limp petals fall off. Some land on Rhian's tear-smeared breasts. She licks the petals off their stem because she senses him, King, watching her and liking it. She knows she's good. She knows he knows. Good enough for him, King. She's proved it. She's found his palace, his open door. She's passed his test. She knows how to not know, now, how to find what can't be found, always.

And then again…

He might make it harder, just to tease her. But she doesn't need to go yet, does she? No one waiting, nagging her with where-you-beens. Why not linger a bit longer? She's even found a few beds upstairs, their swollen pillows and blankets a virgin white under an untouched layer of mould. Let mouldy sheets swallow her, is what she longs for now, breathe it in, lick it off, and sleep, sleep in his bed until he, King, comes. She got everything here. There's no need to leave. So, why not stay a bit longer? Why not – stay?

Rhian hears a creaking sound and turns. She's in the room next to the hall again and can see the front door from here. It's closing by itself.

'Oh, how wrong I was,' Rhian thinks. 'Only now I've passed his test. Now that the door is closing...'

She watches the door shutting ever so slowly, watches with a breathless smile, can't wait for the final click.

'Oi! Love? Yew awrigh'?' someone shouts.

And then it's all gone.

Rhian turns around in horror. The night's cold, the gale's wet and vicious, and she's soaked. She's outside the park's cast-iron fence, stroking something that's choked by layers of ivy and mosses and lichens. And there's a big bloke stumbling towards her. The one who called out to her and ruined it all.

'Fuckin' 'ell... Tha' yew Rhi?' he shouts.

Jamie's so drunk he can hardly stand. He needs the fence to come closer. One look in his face tells Rhian he's been drinking for her.

Oh, how she hates him. He's ruined it all. He's spoilt it for her, he's spoilt it. Of course it's Jamie who got to ruin it.

'Yew spoilt it!' she wants to shout. 'Yew spoilt it!'

He's stopped in front of her. He stoops a bit and takes her face in his clumsy hands as carefully as he can. Warm he is, very warm. In what could be Wookie-speak, he fights for her with the sharp sword of drunken despair. He wants her back! He needs her badly, and even through the thick fog of countless pints and chasers, he can see she needs him too, if she knows it or not. She's cold and thin and nearly see-through, like a wraith.

'Yew gorrw take me back love,' he wails. It's not an order, it's a plea.

'Yewer not the King,' someone else inside Rhian says.

'But – but yewer my queen,' Jamie blurts out.

He can't stand anyhow, so he gets on his knees to pledge silent allegiance, confirmed by a burp.

Slowly, Rhian gives Jamie a nod. A bit of a forced nod, forced perhaps by her own sudden Investiture. She doesn't know. She reckons they'll have to work something out then. Her and him, – um, Jamie. She'll just stop thinking about it. Or maybe she'd better keep thinking about it.

She tries to smile, and Jamie tries too. He gets back up and takes her hand, and they stumble away together, quite determined to live happily ever after. Just like kings and queens do.

Shade

Eileen Dewhurst

Among the men and women spilling out of the Hercules, and onto the hot tarmac of an Akrotiri night, was Flight Lieutenant Dan Fielding. Like all the others clutching kitbags and mobile phones, his tour of duty was over and he was heading for home, to his wife Trish and daughter Pip, aged two. All of these people including Dan would be spending the next week here in Cyprus, relaxing, recuperating, preparing for the picking up of a previous life back home.

The next day Dan hired a car from a jovial Cypriot with a desk in the Officer's Mess.

'You'll be wanting air conditioning,' he said.

'I don't know.' Dan replied, thinking more of an open top, or at least open windows.

'Air conditioning is best. This is the hottest time. You'll be glad of it. You'll see.'

And he was. As the day moved on, the air became thick with heat. His shirt clung to his back and perspiration sprang up wherever his skin made contact with another surface. He'd thought he'd become acclimatised to heat at the field hospital, where hot, dry air rasped in the throat and made for regular encounters with dust devils. This heat was different. This was the heat that grew flamboyant flowers and oversized insects; a lavish heat, he thought, luscious and somehow disturbing. The air conditioning transformed the inside of the car into a capsule of cool air, verging on cold. He kept the windows shut and drove out and away from the base, and the beaches where there would be tourists, and towards the hills. He wasn't quite ready for crowds, for normality, for drinking in bars or shopping. So he drove and watched the road and tried to think of home.

After a while, frustrated with the main road and its slow procession of coaches and dusty pickup trucks, he took a side road and found himself driving through dense olive groves. The light changed. Filtered in through a mesh of silver green foliage, it made for patterns on the tarmac, for a dance of light and shade among the trees. He slowed the car. The trees were old, ancient even. No two the same. Gnarled trunks and branches twisted into contortions of woody limbs locked in embrace. Or battle. He shivered in the air conditioning and drove on.

At the end of the olive groves he drove out onto a hillside. Way down, below the level of the road he could see a village. No signs to give a name or direction, only a track, not quite overgrown, heading towards it. He turned the car. The closer he came, the more it became obvious the place was deserted, buildings shuttered, windows barred or broken. A small church with a rounded dome and a bell tower stood just beyond the houses. He parked beneath the branches of a large eucalyptus and opened the door. Even in the generous shade, the heat hit him like a body blow. The church would be cool. If it was open. From the tangle of wild thistles and blood red poppies crowding the graveyard, Dan suspected no one had been here for quite a time. In the top corners of the few gravestones just visible above the tall grass were faded photographs of the buried, a youthful moment captured, shining black hair, red lips, smiles full of life. Not as they would have looked in their deaths or in their dying. He'd had enough of death and dying. Flashbacks and nightmares were not things Dan suffered from, not in the way some of his colleagues, or most of the patients he'd ever treated did. He dealt with shattered limbs and shot away flesh much as a skilled carpenter might repair a broken chair. But still. Sometimes, he thought of things.

The church was locked. It had one window, barred with heavy iron rods. If he balanced on a rock and stretched to his full height, he could hang on to a narrow sill and just about see through the bars. Whatever was inside was obscured by a film over the glass, clouding it, like the milky sheen of a cataract. It was like looking into the eyes of a blind person. He stepped back to level ground and took a long swallow from his water bottle. Water, he thought. A simple thing. Clean and clear. Uncomplicated. He took one more swallow and turned to go.

Although Dan's business was mending bodies not fighting them, the basic combat training he'd been put through had taught him the art of awareness, how to focus on one thing, the sewing up of an abdomen, the drawing up of morphine, at the same time as being acutely aware of what else was going on around him. Being alert to the subtle signs of danger could be a life saver. And right at that moment, Dan felt the skin on the back of his neck tingle. He was being watched. He was sure of it. He took off his sunglasses and scanned the surroundings, the church, the graves, the blank faces of the empty houses. Nothing moved; the light shone unnaturally bright in the intense heat. Of course, there would be snakes here and feral cats, he thought. Lizards. Buzzards. Naturally, he would be observed. Nonetheless, he walked back to the car quickly, his footsteps moving up a gear, resisting the impulse to look upwards to the bell tower. Only when he was inside the car with the ignition and the air-conditioning turned on, did he look back over his shoulder at the rounded dome shining in the sunlight. He allowed himself a laugh. Too many films. Too many nights in the mess tent watching old westerns. What was he expecting? A de-frocked priest at the bell tower. A man with a gun? He drove back to the base. He was almost there when he realised he'd left his sun glasses behind.

That evening the Wing Commander invited him round for a supper party.

'Never mind post trauma debriefing' he said. 'A good shindig is what you need.'

The Wing Commander's bungalow was already buzzing with people when Dan arrived with his bottle of red wine. It was clear that the Wing Commander and his wife took their entertainment duties seriously and thoroughly enjoyed this side of the job. The other side of the job was managing the running of the hospital and the carrying out of reconstructive facial surgery. Dan understood this; he got it completely, the necessity of hard play, to counter the long hours of work, keeping the balance. He could fling himself into the swing of a party as much as anyone. The food was good but the wine provided by the Wing Commander was better. None of it was local. It arrived on the Hercules from the UK. A swap the Wing Commander said for the cargoes of recharged personnel.

The Wing Commander's wife was called Alice and she made a point of looking after Dan.

'Come on, you'll be needing a top up,' she said refilling the glass which had been emptied and refilled more times than he could remember. The supper guests spread themselves around the house as the evening wore on; some in the kitchen talked about the football results from home, some sprawled on the deep sofas in the Wing Commander's lounge discussing the education of their children, yet more sat around outside on the veranda, braving the mosquitoes and the cockroaches and laughing loudly about everything and anything. No one spoke about where they'd just been or about the things they'd seen.

The music Alice put on gave her age away. Dance music from the eighties.

'Dance with me,' she instructed. And he did, badly, stumbling a little and causing her to giggle like a girl. He didn't mind. It seemed an age since he'd danced with a woman. Trish and Pip were still half a continent away. The Wing Commander was on the veranda with the mosquitoes and two Americans. Dan allowed his arm to slide around Alice's waist and his hand to move upwards towards her breast. She stepped aside quickly.

'Please, don't,' she said, sharply, and he blinked. Before he could apologise, she slipped away to top up the glasses of the people on the sofas.

'Try this,' he heard her say. And the room swam very slightly out of focus.

The next day Dan drove back to the deserted village to find his sunglasses. It wasn't as easy as he'd supposed. So many olive groves. So hard to remember which one. All the roads looked the same. He pulled up outside a tourist shop at the side of the road and asked an old and heavily wrinkled woman in a black dress where he might find an abandoned village with a domed church and was told in good English that there were many abandoned villages here. Some had been made too dangerous by floods and landslides, others deserted during the war, the one way back in 1974. She pointed in the general direction of north and said to take a left turn about two kilometres further on.

He found it, his road through the olive trees. It was familiar, as if he'd always known it. Ah, he thought, here you are. Leaving his car beneath the eucalyptus tree he walked back to the church. There were his glasses lying on the stone beneath the barred window. He picked them up and then, thinking to have one last look, stepped up onto the stone and peered inside. Kneeling at the altar was a woman praying. He went around to the big wooden door and turned the handle. The door opened. Air, colder by some degrees than the air conditioning in the car rushed out to meet him. He stepped inside and was instantly in another world, a cold world, flooded by the sudden influx of the daylight that followed him in. The space was cluttered, crammed with objects, wooden benches, plastic chairs, a table covered in a faded lace table cloth, vases and long dead flowers. It resembled more the living room of an old lady who liked lace and bric a brac. Lace was everywhere, over the backs of the chairs, hanging off the plaster saints. The altar space was curtained with it.

At first the woman was oblivious of his presence. She remained at the foot of the altar, hands clasped, face tilted towards a crucifix on the wall. He gave a little cough to let her know he was there. She turned. Even in the strange half-light he could see she was beautiful. An oval face framed in a lace headscarf that couldn't disguise the shining black hair beneath. Full red lips, slightly parted, eyes that would have been lovely had it not been for the terror that shone in them. He stepped back; hands raised, palms outwards.

'Don't worry,' he called. 'I'm just visiting. I didn't mean to frighten you. I'm so sorry.' The woman, or was she just a girl, he couldn't tell because she'd fallen back on her haunches and lifted her hands to cover her face. He could have turned around and walked away. He could have stepped back into his car and driven off, back to his life. But he couldn't leave her like this. How could he be the cause of such terror? He moved forwards, crooning, it's all right, I won't hurt you. The woman, the girl, or was it a child, it was hard to tell in the half light, was making soft, high pitched sounds. He'd heard a rabbit make such sounds once when it had been corned by his dog.

'It's okay,' he said. 'It's okay.'

She was speaking now, in a language he couldn't understand, and then she took her hands away from her face and said in clear but broken English, 'Please don't, please don't…'

He imagined her stare was directed at him, but then he realised it wasn't. Her eyes were fixed on something or someone behind him. He felt the air move in a cold rush at his back and he turned quickly to see who or what had come in through the open door. There was nothing, only the table with the dead flowers, the clutter of chairs and their lacy covers, and then the door slammed shut and the only light remaining was the thin stream filtered through the lace at the window. He swore and stumbled towards the door, pulled on it, turned the handle, pulled on it again. It wouldn't shift. He turned back to where the woman was and she'd gone. Nothing. No sign that anyone had been here, no dent in the cushion before the altar, no footprints in the dust on the floor. Only the sound, soft and desolate, of whimpering.

It took Dan all of five minutes stumbling in the semi dark to discover the steps leading to the bell tower. It took several more to realise there was no other way out. Below him the olive trees stretched away, a silver green sea, moving in invisible currents of air. It was some time before he understood that the sounds he could hear were not coming from the deep belly of the church.

The people boarding the aircraft bound for Brize Norton early on a bright morning clutched their kitbags and their mobile phones. Dan was given a seat at the front where there would be plenty of room for his extended leg and the plaster cast on his broken ankle. He'd spoken on the phone to Trish and briefly to Pip. 'Daddy's coming home.'

The plane's engines roared and the world outside the window began to blur.

Moments later they were flying high above the clouds. Way below, the blue sea sparkling, the olive groves dark shadows on the hillsides. Dan looked along the row of young airmen, some with arms in slings, others sitting back, eyes tight shut and wondered how many of them could hear it too?

Caretakers

Jo Mazelis

'Human beings are 70 per cent water. The brain is roughly 85 per cent water...'

She is gazing at the lecturer, trying to fight back a yawn. She is so tired her eyes are tearing up. She searches her bag, but no pen. Just a dried up electric lime highlighter. She looks around at the students near her, mouths the word 'pen', makes a squiggle in the air to signify her want. Cold eyes study her, frown, then dismiss her as if she is merely a clown, a puppeteer whose hand is suddenly naked and meaningless.

She leans forward in her chair and stretches out to tap Lolly's shoulder. As he turns, she catches, from beneath her armpit, the strong scent of sweat. Lowers her arm quickly.

'Pen,' she whispers urgently.

Lolly raises his eyebrows, turns back, riffles in his bag then produces a biro. She has to lean over to take it. Her sweat is greasy smelling, like pork and onions.

When the lecture finishes just before lunch, she does not follow the other students to the refectory, but goes home to shower.

Last night she couldn't sleep. All because of the wet footprints she saw, running in a line from the bathroom to the fireplace in her bedroom. The footprints were far smaller than her own. Child-sized naked heel and toe marks, damp on the floorboards and carpet, quickly evaporating to nothing.

The other houses on her street are a mixture of 1930s mock Tudor semis, new apartment blocks and terraced cottages. Hers is the oldest, a Georgian landowner's pile, double-fronted, whitewashed, tall sash windows and six bedrooms. She lives here alone, half ashamed of her good luck in possessing such a house, half afraid that it will somehow be taken from her, invaded, despoiled. She has lived here for over four months. Since September, when she moved in, disbelieving, everything she owned in an old suitcase and a black bin bag. Everything she owned – not forgetting the house and all its contents: the antique furniture, the mahogany and horsehair, the ivory and silks and ormolu, the oil paintings and watercolours, the butler's pantry with its silverware, its cut glass and Clarice Cliff tea sets.

The house was left to her by her great uncle. It was a slap in the face to his children and five grandsons, her own parents and his housekeeper (who may or may not have been his mistress for the preceding fifty years).

'Don't go and live in that awful house,' her mother said. 'Just sell it.' But it was near to the college and she felt compelled somehow, duty-bound.

She puts her bag on the rosewood table in the hall and hangs her jacket on the coat-stand with its carved menagerie of real and mythical creatures, a stag, a unicorn, frogs and lizards with inlaid eyes of ebony, amber and jet. Kicks off her shoes at the base of the stairs and goes up, two steps at a time.

On the landing she stops and searches the floor for signs of footprints. Nothing. She draws closer and kneels to inspect the area for the barest trace of a dark or water-beaded mark.

She glances into her bedroom. Nothing there. Then goes into the bathroom and locks it before disrobing. Turns on the ancient shower and steps under its spluttering, thundering waters. Washes herself, then stands, turning this way and that, luxuriating in the liquid heat. She feels at peace. Cleansed and transcendent. Not reborn, but returned to the womb, to the state of being where there are no edges or boundaries. She lingers, eyes closed, hair plastered flat against her skull, down her back.

She does not go back to college that day. Or the day after that, a Friday. Spends hours curled up on the sofa, the TV on. Thinks that she could go on like this. Forever and forever. If she wasn't so lonely.

On Monday she goes back to college. No one has noticed her absence. They ignore her as before.

After the seminar, she goes to the refectory and does not, as she has in the past, attempt to sit at a table with her fellow students. But they, as bad luck would have it, occupy the table behind her. She can hear every tedious word of their conversation. None of which she wants to hear. Until…

'Did you hear about Lolly?'

'No. What?'

'He's just like, totally broke.'

'Really?'

'Yeah. His father's supposed to pay his rent. But he hasn't, so Lolly's being chucked out.'

'Oh my God!'

'So he owes like nearly a thousand, but his father won't help him and he can't go home.'

'What's he going to do?'

There is no audible answer to this, perhaps the speaker merely shrugged.

They change the subject. She stops listening. Finishes her food, gets up and walks away, very deliberately not looking at them. Someone laughs, perhaps at her.

She sees Lolly crossing the big hall, weaving between tables packed with students. He has a plate of chips and a white plastic cup of water. Nothing else. Lolly is a big guy, tall, broad-shouldered, but also overweight. His lumberjack shirt is crumpled and he looks like he needs a shave. Tucked away, near the fire exit is a narrow corridor with three small tables, he heads there and she follows. At one of the tables, sitting on the chair as if waiting for a companion is a large nylon rucksack, on the floor beside it are two carrier bags, and a sleeping bag. Lolly slumps into the seat opposite.

She pulls over a chair and sits.

'Lolly,' she says.

'Don't call me that.'

'But everyone…'

'My name is Lawrence.'

He averts his gaze and begins eating.

'So… Someone said you were looking for a place…'

'Oh yeah? Well someone is talking out of their ass. Ok?'

'Oh. I'm sorry. I heard that…and then here you are with your rucksack and this bag and…'

He looks her in the eye; his expression is flat, guarded. She waits. He says nothing.

'I was going to say. You know, if you're stuck. Between places? Then you could stay at mine. For a while. If you want…'

'For real? Are you for real?' A grin is starting to break out all over his face. He's handsome when he smiles.

'Yeah, for real.'

When their last lecture finished at three she and Lolly lingered until the rest of the class had drifted away, before setting off together – him almost a giant made even larger by his huge rucksack. She, at least a head and a half shorter, had to run every few paces to keep up with him.

They didn't talk. There was no conversational opening which wouldn't have been painful for either; he didn't want to talk about the situation with his father, she was ashamed of owning a big Georgian house set in an acre of land, he did consistently well at college, she was scraping along most of the time. Everybody at college liked him, though he seemed to make no effort to be liked, while she tried desperately to charm and ingratiate herself, but got nowhere.

The Lolly/Lawrence thing was interesting, she thought

as they turned into her street, he hated being called Lolly but said nothing. The man they all liked, Lolly, Big Loll, Lolls who was big and a tad overweight, but handsome and affable, was their own invention. The jolly giant, he was safe, good at walking home girls too drunk to look after themselves.

In a similar fashion they must have created a version of her that bore little resemblance to reality. This person was spiky and mean, jealous of the other girls.

Maybe as she and Lawrence got to know one another better they would have a conversation about this and then, understanding everything about her, he would become her envoy, making others see her in a whole new light.

As they began down the drive to the house, he gave no sign of surprise at its majesty. But then he had no idea of her relationship to the house, she might have been a live-in skivvy for all he knew and lived in a caravan around the back.

'Here it is.'

He stepped in and looked around.

She had almost stopped seeing how grand the hall was, but now she could see it reflected in his gaze.

'How many people live here?'

'Just me.'

'Just…you?'

'I'm the caretaker.'

He seemed relieved to hear that. She smiled. How easily the lie had come to her.

'Well…' she began, but then she sensed a presence near

her, very close by, and a fleeting touch of something cool and very slightly moist on the back of her hand. A quick glimpse and there they were, fading and drying already, two bare footprints that seemed to be waiting, hungry for attention.

'You okay?' he said.

'Yes, just tired. Let's find you a room, eh?'

When they were halfway up the stairs, he said, 'You won't get in trouble will you?'

'It's fine,' she said. 'As long as nothing is damaged or whatever... We're not going to have wild parties are we?'

'God, no.'

'Okay, that's my room,' she indicated the closed door opposite the bathroom. 'How about you have this room, next to it?' She led him into the master bedroom. It was a big room, high-ceilinged, 22 feet by 18, with three tall sash windows, each with the original wooden shutters. There were long yellow brocade curtains that pooled on the floor and were faded in places. The bed with its walnut headboard stood in the centre of the room, the bare mattress was indecently pink and shiny.

Lawrence put his bags on the floor, then unrolled the sleeping bag and laid it out along one half of the bed. It was one of those high altitude sleeping bags, a black cocoon that was narrower at the feet than the upper body, like a sarcophagus.

'There's plenty of bedding; pillows, blankets, sheets, eiderdowns,' she said.

'This will be fine' he said.

'But...'

It looked so temporary and so out of place, that sleeping bag on the luxurious satin of the mattress. He does not mean to stay, she thought, he can't wait to escape.

He busied himself with his stuff, going through the bags, not unpacking but searching for something. Eventually he came to a limp looking roll of faded purple towel and a striped nylon wash bag.

'Would it be ok if I had a wash? Need to shave,' he said, rubbing a hand over his bristly chin, so that a faint rasping sound could be heard.

'Yes. Yes, of course. The bathroom's just here. Have a shower.'

He went in and she hovered at the open door.

'We'll have to sort out some money for bills,' he said, as if in answer to her watching him.

'Plenty of time,' she said,

He turned on the shower and held a hand under, testing it, then steam began to gather and rise and he withdrew his hand. Smiling awkwardly, he crossed the room and closed the door in her face.

At college, as the days went by, he behaved towards her exactly as he had always done. He did not sit beside her in lectures, nor share a table in the refectory. They did not walk to college together and after the last lecture of the day he always seemed to be caught up in a laughing conversation with one group of students or another.

To punish him she had not yet given him his own set of keys.

Yet each evening they ate together. She had an allowance, she explained, for expenses, and this covered all the bills, even food. She bought ready meals from Marks and Spencer and heated them in the oven, decanting them onto the best plates and adding flourishes like side salads and steam-in-the-bag vegetables. There was always wine too, though he professed at first not to like it. She put fresh flowers on the table and lit the candles in the silver candelabra.

They started, from desultory beginnings, to have real conversations, though the focus was always weighted towards him, she, having much to hide, used a subtle sleight of hand to keep herself in the shadows.

Only two years before, he had been an outstanding athlete; excelling at cricket, rugby, long distance running, swimming and basketball. Then he'd had his 'accident' while rock climbing.

'But I was lucky,' he said, and she thought it would be luckier not to fall at all, though did not say this. 'I could have been paralysed. I could have been dead. Instead, a year and a half in hospital and I'm as right as rain. Just out of shape. Look!' He pulled his wallet from his back pocket, took out a newspaper clipping. There he was, a god of a man in Speedo swimming trunks, every muscle toned and lean; pecs, biceps, abs, quads. His face, stripped of the plump cheeks and double chin, was that of a Hollywood film star, a young dimpleless Robert Mitchum crossed with Jake Gyllenhaal.

She passed it back to him quickly, afraid to linger over this image, to betray her feelings.

He'd also revealed more about the quarrel with his father who'd left the family when Lawrence was too young to remember. The father who had promised to pay his rent, but hadn't and wouldn't answer his calls.

Term broke up for Easter and without saying anything to her, he disappeared for three weeks. She had bought enough food for the two of them for the coming week and a turkey crown for Easter Sunday and a chocolate egg each.

In his room the sleeping bag still lay on the bare mattress and there were a few of his things scattered about, but his rucksack was gone. In the weeks before this she had barely noticed the little naked footprints. Perhaps with him there she had been too distracted to notice them. Perhaps he scared them away? Whatever it was, throughout Easter they were back with a vengeance. She saw them in the bathroom, the hall and landing, in the kitchen, bedroom and living room. Very often they were side by side next to her own feet and sometimes seemed to disperse her loneliness, at others to distil it, making it far more potent.

The doorbell rang on the last Friday of the holidays at eight o'clock.

She opened the door to find Lawrence on the threshold. He was tanned and seemed to have lost the last of the excess fat. He wore flip flops, khaki shorts and a white T-shirt.

'Hi,' he said, hefting the rucksack from his back and onto the floor. Not wanting to look at his face, she found herself concentrating on his feet. There were grains of sand still visible between his toes. She hated him for that, for making her remember long ago summer days when she had come home from the beach, sand everywhere and the sea pulsing in her head, the waves still visible when she shut her eyes to sleep.

'Hello,' she said as coldly as she could, but he seemed oblivious.

'Think I'll have a shower,' he said. 'Is there anything to eat?'

She turned sharply on her heel, went to the kitchen and crashed about with pots and pans, browning meat, chopping onions, garlic, mushrooms, chillies.

She heard the creak of the floorboards overhead and the rattle of the pipes as the shower was turned on.

She boiled rice and poured half a bottle of Claret into the sauce. Drank the other half, then opened a second bottle.

The little feet beside her seemed to wobble unsteadily. Her little ghost was drunk, she thought, as she sloshed more wine into a tumbler and drank deeply.

'Smells great!' He was standing in the doorway, his hair still wet, his face gleaming, a pair of loose white linen trousers covering his lower half, while his chest was bare. She turned away quickly, afraid to let her gaze linger over that taut, muscled skin, the black hair that gathered in the centre of his chest and ran in a line over his flat stomach.

'Can I have a glass?' he asked and when she looked up, she saw that he had put a T-shirt on.

He began to potter about, putting cutlery on the table in the adjoining room, lighting the candles. Then he put music on; soft swirling pipes and insistent drums, the sound of a night far away in Morocco or Tunisia. Hand claps and a woman's voice, a rhythmic ululating lament.

She slopped the food onto plates, splashes of tomato everywhere, rice spilled on the stove top, the floor, the counter.

'Can I help?' he asked.

She shook her head, unable to speak. A plate in each hand and the wine bottle tucked under her arm.

'Oops,' he said, coming closer, reaching behind her so that she thought for one moment he was going to put his arms around her. 'You left the gas on.' The pan that had held the rice was blackening and fizzing.

She lurched unsteadily forward and made it through to the dining room without a mishap, tipping the bottle so a little wine sloshed out on to the tablecloth. He filled their glasses and she drained hers immediately. Being this drunk, she thought, is like being in deep water. At the bottom of the ocean with all that weight above you.

'This is great!' he said. 'I've really missed this.'

She half closed one eye in order to focus on him across the table.

'The food?' she said, slurring horribly.

'The food, the house, you and me chilling. Everything.'

By candlelight, even through her drunken haze, he seemed to shine like a Greek god, Apollo or Eros or Dionysus. She tried to shrug, wishing to show him that she couldn't care less if he was there or not. She should just let herself drown she thought, pour more wine down her open throat, let the tides consume her.

Her glass was wet as if a small damp hand had touched it. All around the table, she seemed to see stumbling little footprints as if a child had run around in giddy circles, revelling in this new sensation, this drunkenness.

'So, where did you go?' he asked.

'Huh?'

'Where did you go while they were here?'

'Who-oo?' she said thinking guiltily of the little ghost.

'The owners. You said they'd be back for the holidays.'

Had she said such a thing? Even sober it was hard to keep track of all her lies.

He was watching her face, waiting for an answer.

'They come and go,' she said. 'Like little ghosts.'

He laughed.

'You're funny,' he said. 'I missed that. I missed you.'

This was too much. She rose to her feet, swayed for a second, then walked, her upper body tipping forward perilously, from the room.

Upstairs, she collapsed on her bed fully clothed, then passed out. In the night she drifted in and out of watery dreams and at times awoke to the sounds of rattling pipes and gurgling water. At dawn, with her bladder full and her head throbbing, she tiptoed to the bathroom, relieved herself and drank handfuls of cool, clear water from the tap. The house was silent and still, the door to his room was closed. He had said he missed her, she remembered; that she was funny. He'd laughed and smiled and lit the candles and put on that mysterious and strangely seductive music.

She stood in the hallway gazing towards his room. Should

she go in there? Silently climb onto the bed beside him? But there was no soft duvet to lift so that she could snuggle under. He would be in his cocoon of a sleeping bag, the mattress beside him, pink and bare, slippery, cold and unyielding.

In the morning she would make up his bed properly, take away that sleeping bag, put it in the wash or at least turn it inside out and put it on the line to air in the spring sunshine.

She might also confess her lies.

She took a few steps closer to his room, wanting to sense his nearness, to hear his breathing. Then smiling to herself, she returned to her room, undressed, got properly into bed and in seconds she was asleep.

She was awoken by the front door slamming shut and ran to the window in time to see Lawrence jogging down the path towards the gates. She could just make out the thin white wires of an MP3 player trailing from his sweatshirt.

She took a long shower, shaving her legs, then applying body lotion. She had neglected herself for too long. She put on her dress she'd found in one of the wardrobes. It was worn soft with age and there was a tear beneath one of the arms, but it was a pretty print and a flattering style.

She made up the bed in the master bedroom and hung his sleeping bag on the line to air. She was in the kitchen waiting for the kettle to boil, when a sudden breeze fluttered at her bare legs, preceding the slammed front door.

'Do you want lunch?' she called.

He came and stood beside her, gently touched her shoulder. 'This is nice. You look pretty in a frock.'

He paused a moment, then kissed her cheek.

'I need a soak,' he said. 'Not used to this much exercise. Won't be long.'

She switched the radio on, turned up the volume and fairly danced about the kitchen, washing lettuce, chopping tomatoes, cucumber, spring onions. She fried mushrooms, leftover potato, onions and ham, then set them to one side, meaning to add the eggs at the last moment. They grew cold in the pan as the minutes went by. She sipped her tea and went to the window, the apple tree was in blossom and the rhubarb was unfurling its giant leaves. His sleeping bag was hanging on the line like a great bat, its wings folded and its head down. Lifeless.

How long had he been upstairs? Too long, she thought, and her heart seemed to flutter inside her chest, to quiver like an insubstantial jellyfish. She raced up the stairs, the bathroom door was shut and no sound came from behind it. As she looked she saw a trail of watery footsteps stepping from the bathroom and crossing the landing. Each print evaporated as a new one appeared.

He did not drown. It had been something to do with his fall from the cliff two years before, a small bleed seeping slowly into his brain that the doctors had missed. There was no water in his lungs, they said, it could have happened at anytime, anywhere, but she knew better. A wild creature such as the one that haunted her house could go anywhere, do anything, it could transmute itself, seep through the skin, invade the veins and arteries of the body, make a lake in the lungs or the heart or the brain. Do its damage then evaporate without a trace. All of us are 70 per cent water. The rest is love and hate.

The View From Up Here

Carly Holmes

I've got your hand, you can't break loose, so don't even bother trying. Just relax and enjoy the ride. Sorry to disappoint but we're going up, not down. Up through the clouds. See how wet they are, and feel how soft. If I dropped you now you'd plunge straight through, straight down, and arrive on earth soaked to the skin and worse. But I've got your hand, I won't let you fall.

Here's where I spin. It's going to make you queasy but it helps with the moving between this week and last, and it's last week that we have to get to. I just need to show you something then I'll leave you alone. Pop you right back on your cliff-top perch with all still ahead of you. Hang on tight. Unless of course you really are determined to end it all and then letting go will be easy.

Not that tight! That's better. Now, if I'm right we should be at last Thursday. Let's go over the edge and see what we find. Shall I speed this up? Give you an idea what it feels like to drop towards the rocks like a dislodged gull egg and no going back?

You can open your eyes now. We're here. Last Thursday. Same cliff, different day. He landed an hour ago and he died twenty minutes later. Not much left of him, is there? It was a long twenty minutes. He'll be found before the tide comes in; the traffic here, though always one-way, is depressingly regular. Ha! And so the weary men and women whose job it is to scrape him up and reassemble the pieces will be dragged from their homes and their complicated lives. They'll curse and grumble but they'll wield their spades with tenderness.

Do you want to know what he was thinking when he jumped? I know what they all think, and it's generally the same. Why not? Too real for you? Too raw? But this is it. Take another look. When flesh hits a hard surface at tremendous speed, that right there is the result.

Okay, let's spin forward just a few hours and go east. About twenty miles, give or take. We've got to rise above the clouds again though, because I need plenty of room, so up, up, up we go. We don't want to be banging into the cliff at a hundred revolutions a minute. Though I'd be fine if we did, it's just you that wouldn't and that would render this whole exercise pointless.

Now, she's making this easy for us, running around the garden. All we have to do is hover. So can you guess who she is? Surely it's obvious? Limbs twitching every which way, mouth stretched thin and wide.

That's right, mother of the deceased. She's just been told. Look at her go! What despair! She'll fall in a moment and that's when it'll hit her. The frantic energy gone and just the pain left. Ouch. There, told you! Over she goes. Someone will come soon and pick her up and take her indoors. Then she'll be placid and hollow. Just a doll with the insides all gone. Do you think she'll ever get them back? My mother hasn't got her insides back yet and it's been a few years since I took them away from her. I visit her occasionally but it does strange things to my form, cold spots and hard spots and things going off kilter. Too much emotional energy. I'm not supposed to have substance, being a ghost, but with her I can feel the old human frame pushing to break through, trying to stiffen my arms to reach out to her. If I stick around for too long I think there's a danger she'll see me, or see what I once was, so I only pop in and out occasionally, and never on the big dates. You know...the anniversaries and suchlike.

Don't worry, just a couple more stops then I'll take you back. I just want you to think things through a bit more. A bit more than I did anyway. A bit more than he did. Not much to ask really, once you've seen the horror movie that keeps on playing for other people after your credits have rolled. Right, back up again, but we can stay below the clouds this time because we're only crossing miles, not time. Have to get above the electricity wires, though, or we'll short-circuit the whole area. I made that mistake once and had to leave the woman I was with, she was in the same frame of mind as you, tangled in the wires forty feet above the ground. Fried to a crisp. Now that had everyone puzzling, I can tell you. The conspiracy theorists had a field day!

This scene lacks the dramatic impact of the last, I know, but take note anyway. It's going to be more difficult to see because I can't touch the ground. Did I tell you that? I'm no longer of this earth and so I'm condemned never to be united with it. I've tried dive bombing it and creeping up on it but as soon as I get within a handful of inches I'm pinged back into the air like a cork from a bottle. You don't realise how much you miss making mud pies until you're deprived of them forever.

So, we'll just hang around here and look through the window. I won't tell you who this one is, it'll spoil the ending, but look at her face. See the anxiety scratched there. Eyes constantly seeking the clock, watching the seconds twitch forwards. Tick-tock, tick-tock. She's waiting, and she's worrying, and the only thing that's stopping her from going out and looking is the babe in the next room.

Seen enough? Then up we go again, and forward a couple of hours, and back to the grieving mother. I like the way you winced then, you're less like me already. That's good.

So behold the bereaved, rocking in her chair. The telephone keeps ringing, the front door keeps opening, people keep talking to her, trying to reach her, but she can't hear them. Memories louder than words. Don't turn your face away, that's cheating. I'll just keep talking anyway.

The front door opens again, and in *he* walks! That got your attention! She doesn't raise her head at first, she doesn't focus, but then she sees, and she hears the gasps around her, and she starts to walk towards him with her hands up in front of her face. He must be real because they all see him too. A dead man walking! A tumble of snapped bones and bloodied flesh put back together and made live again. How can that be? He's bruised and confused. He opens his mouth to ask something and then she's on him and he's driven backwards by the force of her body and her joy.

Are you looking? Heart-warming, isn't it? Imagine getting the chance to regain the one you've lost. Imagine that. And now in pile the relatives and the friends and the gruesome spectators. We'll pull away now, I don't want you to piece the puzzle together yet, and arrive at the ending before you've actually arrived at the ending.

And back to the clouds. Shall we dance for a while? I spend hours on the clouds above the cliff, our cliff, just dancing and grooving. It does tend to distract me from my task, though, and a fair few with intentions like yours slip past me and over the edge. He, the dead man, was one I was aware of and had to let go, though I wanted to intervene. I always want to intervene, once they've got my attention. But his was a cautionary tale too perfect, all the twists and turns and drama.

You've sure got some moves! Show me that jive again. I love it! Let's go from the top just one more time, then I'll spin us to the last couple of tableaux and get out of your hair. I'm sure you're sick of me by now.

Do you recognise this street? Are you okay? Lie back and breathe deeply. You'll be fine. So, we're several hours before 'The Return of the Prodigal Son', now, and his day hasn't even started yet. Here he is, he's just cut down that alleyway and he's in a rush. In slips a man behind him. Let's get closer and see what happens.

Ooh! Bet that hurt! And he's down like a sack of spuds.

He'll have a lump there the size of an egg, tomorrow. Away with his wallet and his briefcase. Even his jacket! But at least the thief has left him his shoes. We'll leave the Prodigal Son to his dreams, we know he's going to be okay because we saw him this very evening. Well, this very evening last Thursday. If you see what I mean? I'm getting my tenses confused but I'm sure you see what I mean.

So we'll stick with the thief. He doesn't look happy does he? The jacket's a perfect fit, though, that should cheer him up. And into the pocket the wallet goes. A pivotal moment. Shall I spin us back a few seconds and replay that? Are you getting how this is going to end yet?

In and out of the shop, and what's that? Looks like whisky to me. He's a thirsty one! And he's left the briefcase open on the street. Litter bug! Oops, nearly dropped you there, sorry. Let me hold you a bit tighter and get us above the houses. Yes, and the pylons! You know where we're going, don't you? I want to reach there first. Let him catch us up when he's good and ready.

Ah, smell that sea breeze! I love the view from up here, which is lucky because I'll be spending eternity taking it in. And here he comes, right on cue. Let's shift over a bit, make room for him. He wants to look over the edge for a while and test his resolve. It's a long way down and no way back up. Is he as desperate as you, do you think? As determined? Or is he just indulging a moment of petty cut-off-my-nose-to-spite-my-face? It never fails to amaze me how casually some people will extinguish their own light, particularly when they've had a couple of snifters.

He'll need some time though, so we'll give him that. We've all been here after all.

I think he's ready to go! Hang onto me, I'm going over with him. I love this bit, when we plummet together face to face. Isn't this great? I can almost feel my once-stomach flipping upside down. Stop screaming! It'll be the last ride you ever take, so why not enjoy it? Just look at him. You don't have to be a ghost to tell what he's thinking right now. Bit late though, isn't it?

Okay, this may jolt a bit, but I'll do my best to slow us down before the dreaded ping throws us back up again.

Woohoo, that was fun! Can we do it again? Oh, you forgot that I can't touch the ground! Did you think you were done for? Take a look at him before we spin out of here. The wallet lying on his chest like a badge of honour. He's still alive, just. Go on, take another look. No? All right, up, up, up we go, and then the final spin back to *now*, and I'll leave you be. No harm done. Not to you anyway. Not yet.

I've had an idea! Why don't we spin forward a few more hours and see how the girlfriend takes the news, once they've sorted out the mix-up with the identities? You forgot about her, didn't you? But she's still out there, watching the clock and hoping and getting ready to fling her arms around her man. *She* won't get a chance to have her insides back. Are you sure? Shame.

Well, here we are, back at the beginning. I'm sure you were nearer the edge when I put you down. So are you going to jump? Go on, I'm dying, ha ha, to hear what you've decided.

Good man! So many ripples, and so much pain, and that's without counting yours. Believe me, what you saw down there hurts like a bastard. Go home now and give her a kiss from me. Whoever she is, whoever's in your life who needs her insides to stay right where they are, give her a kiss from me. I do miss the kissing.

Do you want to know another thing? I'm going to miss *you*. I really enjoyed the company and the larking around. I was hoping that we'd have an eternity of hanging out together.

So if you ever change your mind, I'll still be here. I'm not going anywhere.

Harvest

Sian Preece

'A writer?' says Mrs Quinn. 'We've had writers before...' and she is so obviously trying to conceal some emotion that I suspect she's had a hard time with them – a spoilt old bachelor fussing about his nursery food, or an arrogant boy who left cigarette burns in the furniture and thought he was Jack Kerouac. I determine to be No Trouble At All.

'A poet,' I add, to get it out in the open. I judge Mrs Quinn to be in her seventies at least, and imagine the memorised museum of *thees* and *thous* and strict rhyme schemes that must represent 'poetry' to her. But she shows none of the usual fear, and just says:

'You'll be quiet here.'

I feel we've reached an understanding.

She shows me the workings of the cottage – the place where the logs are kept, the tricksy half-turn that brings soft, cold water to the single tap – and conveys, by a series of delicate hints, how not to clog the toilet. There's a small wood-burning stove in the vast fireplace, and a smoke-stained mantle above hinting at larger, more glorious fires in the past.

'The local standing stones were scavenged to build the house,' says Mrs Quinn. 'People didn't understand then. About history. It could have been the Welsh Stonehenge! But to be fair, they raided the old church too – the garden wall is built from Norman stones – and, see, that little round window, set into the wall.'

There is still glass in it, no bigger than a saucer, a central cross of lead letting a thin yellow light into the dark room. The other windows are uncurtained, but there's a thick tapestry to pull around the bed at night, a lumpy horsehair single bunk opposite the fireplace. It smells of damp and woodsmoke and other people's sleep.

'There's still an ancient burial chamber,' says Mrs Quinn, 'a cairn, if you walk into the woods a bit. I've left some leaflets…' There they are, fanned across the rough table on which I am to eat and work for the next few weeks. 'Neolithic. Or is it some other…Stone Age? Anyway, very old. It's all in the leaflets.' She taps them with a finger.

Already proprietorial, wanting her out so I can take possession of the cottage, I walk her to the end of the garden where she shows me the tall, thin shed outside the gate, like a sentry box, where she will be leaving my meals each morning. My washing too if I want it done, for a small extra sum…

'I'll be fine,' I tell her. I tend to wear the same clothes for weeks when I'm on a project. (This, I don't tell her. People imagine you smell, and they may be right.)

'Leave a note if you want anything,' she says. 'Or come down to the farmhouse if you're lonely.'

She smiles, and I smile back; I won't be.

'Thank you,' I say.

She sets off to the end of the track, where her grandson will come and pick her up on the quad bike. I see her wave to him, down in the valley below, and she stands to wait for him with that countryside placidity, not fidgeting or checking her watch. She wears no watch. I was right to come here. I wish I could stay to watch her ride off, daintily side-saddle on the pillion seat, but I turn back to the cottage and embark on my project of being No Trouble.

People do expect trouble from poets – breakdowns and crises, jealous love affairs. At parties they ask hopefully if I have 'an over-active imagination', and seem disappointed when I say that I do not. Flaubert wrote to a female admirer: *Be regular and orderly in your life like a bourgeois, so that you may be violent and original in your work.* I agree with this philosophy. So I see to my comforts, as particular as a cat, and like a cat I have no fear of dark nights or lonely forests. The drama happens on the page.

When I can be sure that Mrs Quinn has gone, I take a small, leg-stretching walk around the garden, tracing its circular perimeter, then come back in to try working at the table until the light fades. I get nothing useful done, but I know this is part of the process, the composting. I am patient. I reheat Mrs Quinn's 'welcome' meal of a lamb stew on the little stove, leave the rinsed pot at the sentry box, and return to the cottage, locking the door, though she said that no one ever comes here. Teeth and face washed in the cold water, I draw the curtain around my bed and prepare for a good night's sleep.

I sleep, but I am annoyed to find, in the morning, that I have dreamed. I know I always have dreams, like anyone, but I usually wake at the right time in my sleep cycle to forget them. I've been disturbed. It's dawn, the birds probably woke me, and I go to the window and look out to the sentry box; I know my dream was set there, but I can remember no more, and it fades.

I can see I'm going to have to rise every day at dawn, if the birds have their way. But this is fine, I like the idea of corresponding to old patterns – bed at dusk, rise with the sun. I think I can find some natural rhythm there that will help.

Nevertheless, the work doesn't go well today. After a few hours I take Mrs Quinn's leaflets and go to look for the burial cairn. It's not far from the cottage, but down a steep hill, I can see how it was missed when they were plundering stones for the house. The leaflet describes its various parts – the chambers where, when the mound was excavated a century ago, they found the bones of forty people, crockery, animal remains. It's a low, open construction, no higher than my waist at any point, and it looks quite sweet, like a den that children would make if they had the patience to pile stone upon stone in such numbers. I like the chambers, each leading off a narrow central corridor. They are snug, like the cells of a honeycomb. Inviting and person-sized. I sit in one like a bath and feel nothing sinister, just the sun's warmth radiating back out from the rock. I wish I knew more about geology, history. There's a large slab at one end that the leaflet suggests, wistfully, may be 'a sacrifice stone', but I think of as The Picnic Table – I've brought the food that Mrs Quinn left this morning, and sit down on the table to eat it.

I was surprised that, though I had risen at dawn, she had still managed to get up before me and leave a small feast in the sentry box – a Thermos of coffee, hard-boiled eggs, bread that is surely home-made. A small pot of honey. When I arrived at the farm, she was checking her beehives, without a veil or gloves, and walked calmly to greet me through a tangle of cottage garden flowers, the dark, buzzing haze of the swarm parting around her. In a neat print frock and tennis shoes, she struck me as a proper farmer's wife, gliding over the mud where I clumped laboriously in my hiking boots.

I shake the crumbs off my lap and set off back home. My work is waiting where I left it on the table. As my eyes adjust to the dark interior, I scowl at it – perhaps I would do better to take it to the cairn tomorrow. I eat a huge, delicious pasty, again bearing the hand of Mrs Quinn, and by dusk my eyes are drooping. I draw the curtain around my little bed.

And dream again. I remember more this time – a figure in the woods – not threatening at all. It comes to the bottom of the garden, by the sentry box, and gazes at the cottage. Is this my Muse? It's a man – quite fitting that I should have a male Muse, if male writers get beautiful women; only fair. He stands by the garden gate, and then he is gone, sliding into the shadows of the forest, as slender and pale as a birch.

I wake with the birds again, and go straight to the window. I see immediately where the dream came from – of course it's the sentry box. I can see this morning how much it looks like a human, the same rough height and heft, standing on the boundary between the garden and the forest. But it's just a shed; I've seen inside it like a magician's box. Nothing there. Just this morning's bread, wholemeal this time, and cheese wrapped in greaseproof paper. Mrs Quinn has been here before me again.

I decide I won't even bother with the table today. I eat the bread and cheese hastily, gather my notebook and pencils, and go straight to the cairn. A scattering of crows billows up as I approach – I wonder if they are expecting me to drop food for them. I know that crows can peck out lambs' eyes, their tongues; the soft body parts. But it's September, the lambs will be grown now, maybe even gone to slaughter already. I think of the stew I ate. I wonder how the Quinns manage, if the offer of washing was a hint, and if I should help them with the small fee for that. But the thought of contacting Mrs Quinn, speaking to her, makes me feel oddly uncomfortable. It's not that I'm shy. Perhaps I am getting ready to write again – that can sometimes feel like you're going down with something, a fever, moving you to isolate yourself like a sick animal.

But I haven't written today. The stone starts to feel cold, the evening drawing in, and I clamber out of my chamber and hurry back to the cottage before it gets dark. When I get there, Mrs Quinn has left a cold chicken, stuffed with herbs. Potato salad. I eat fast, almost asleep as I finish the last mouthfuls. This evening I leave the bed curtain drawn back. To see the dawn, of course.

Tonight the man in my dream seems closer to the house, though I can see he is still outside the gate. I feel sure he can't get in. He gives every impression of wanting me to go to him, like a dog that wants you to follow it to the door, outside, for a walk. I wonder if this represents my work in some way, my subconscious kicking in; or if it's just the change of diet muddling my dreams, Mrs Quinn's food…

Bread again, and honey this morning. A fat slice of butter, still cold from the fridge. I suddenly think: it must be Mrs Quinn's grandson – the one with the quad bike – he must come up here before dawn, leaving the food. Of course he does. And it is he who is coming into my dreams, waking me, disturbing the birds at dawn. A man at the bottom of the garden, indeed. A *boy*. I laugh at myself.

I put the food on the table, placing it meanly on my

notebook, hoping it stains. My book is no friend to me these days. I can't even bring myself to pick up my pencils. This is new for me; I've never been afraid to write. I bust through blocks, don't believe in them. And besides, I feel the fever, the work brewing. This is usually an exciting time for me; it's just not resolving itself into words. It's baffling. I decide suddenly to leave my book, just take my breakfast to the cairn and spend the day there, thinking this through, or not thinking, letting it work through me. The idea strikes me as so excitingly *right*, I am almost running by the time I get there, my rucksack bouncing on my back. The crows seem less afraid of me today. I throw them a crust of my bread, and they're too clever to come while I'm there, but I see their crafty corvid faces, remembering the food for later on.

The chamber is like an old armchair to me now, cosy and inviting. I try different chambers as the sun goes overhead, choosing each one to turn me, like a flower, to face the light, the warmth. I tune in to the sounds of the forest. I even think I can hear the stones themselves, the beetles scuttling up and down the trees…a spider runs across me, like a finger trailed over my face, and I jump up. The sun has moved. It's time to be back home.

Getting in, I see my notebook idle on the table and, without slowing my pace, I snatch it up and stuff it into the stove. My hand is shaking as I strike the matches, one, two, putting them to the pages, watching the dark spasm and curl of them. Smiling at the light and heat. I even put the pencils in, see the paint peel off, a flaring chemical flame. It feels like I am getting something of worth from them at last. Words are just clumsy compared to those noises – the greedy eating of the fire, the sated sigh of smoke. I see the leaflets for the cairn and feed them in too. Then anything in the house that has writing on it – I cannot bear to see it, not the labels on the food cans nor the newspapers twisted into spills, nor even the trade name on the toilet (I prise the plastic label off with a knife). I rip and burn and douse in water, and what will not burn or drown, I take outside and bury, scraping a grave in the earth with a flat rock from the garden wall.

This is what I needed to do! No written words, bossy and inadequate, coming between me and reality. Not even spoken words. Just sound, pure. I try to copy the flickering of the fire and the water, producing them from somewhere unused and unaccustomed in my throat – *ahhs* and *kkks*, striking the vowels and consonants against each other like flint. Sparking meaning. I am the instrument, and I am the noise itself. I sing and howl, experimenting with sound, until the dusk falls and my voice breaks. Then I cram the food into my mouth without even bothering to heat it. I fall asleep on the bed, bloated and fully clothed.

All night, for every second of my sleep, the man waits on the edge of the forest. He knows how I have changed. He opens his mouth to speak, but I hear nothing, and he is too far for me to see his lips move. Though I run to the door as soon as I wake, run to the gate, to the start of the woods, he is not there. And this time, I was so sure he would be.

I eat my breakfast straight from the sentry box where it has been left. The Thermos is there, with its orange tartan pattern, its logo on the side. Incensed anew by the writing, the intrusion of the letters, I take a stone from the wall and I scratch at the paint until the word is gone, just shining metal underneath. The coffee inside is still hot, thick with creamy milk. I pour it hungrily into my mouth, throw the empty flask back into the shed. The rest of the day's food is there – a pie, some apples, a ginger cake – and I eat it all where I stand, cramming and swallowing, barely chewing, licking the greaseproof paper clean.

The crows hardly move as I arrive at the cairn, just a desultory flap to acknowledge my arrival. They have taken yesterday's bread. Stumbling in the long grass I fall to my knees, short of the chambers, and it seems right to be on the ground. I crawl towards them. The grass is loud in my ears. I hear the song of the ants, the hum of the earthworms – the cold, moist current that moves their muscle, rasping their clammy bodies through the mud. I do not know how I have ignored these sounds for so long, wasted my time with words. I hoot and moan, and the noise resonates in me like a bell. I put my head into each chamber, going frantically from one to the next, trying to find the perfect pitch, the perfect vibration.

I don't know how long I stay there, making that sound, open-mouthed, trying to hone it. I just feel the cooling shawl of dusk, and know I have to get back to the house now before the dark, the cold. Movement is effort, heavy, like running in a dream. But I get home, I find my bed, dive into it and lie still to sleep.

Suddenly I realise I have to try to stay awake. If I can stay awake, I can meet the man. I have to tell him about this, to show him. My song. He has been waiting for me to find it. He has been waiting in the night, and I've been looking for him in the day.

Drowsy, I go to the tap and drink glass after glass of cold water, filling my stomach, trying to shock myself awake. I haven't eaten since my binge this morning, and I think: God, so much food! I hadn't realised it. Mrs Quinn has been feeding me like a hungry farmboy, like a pregnant sow. Bowls of potatoes, slick with butter; a loaf to myself, a whole cake. Why did I eat it? I never eat this much. I slide to the floor, exhausted with my own weight. The darkness makes me nod, my head going down to my chest like a bird's. I jerk it up again. And again.

And I sleep…

A noise wakes me. I'm sore from lying on the floor, it's still dark outside, I can't see. Then there's another bang, short, truncated. A piece of glass from the old church window flies into the room. Someone is throwing stones at it, someone is outside.

The man. He is at the gate. I think I will reach him there, my bare feet flying over the cold grass, but when I get to it, he is gone – no, there, in the woods. I run after him, but he stays always the same distance ahead of me, just at the corners, then gone, till I see him again through the trees.

The clearing is lit with a harvest moon, a singing moon some call it, fat and low and red. He stops by the cairn now, and I see how tall he is, but so thin, so wretchedly emaciated that it doesn't matter that he is naked. I step closer. There is no smell from him, no warmth, none of the normal elecricity of life. I reach out to touch him, and he shakes his head, no, puts his hand to his mouth. To reassure him, I open my own mouth and the sound that comes out is purer than ever, as clean and clear as the moonlight itself. He steps back, shakes his head, tries to cover his ears; then he holds out his arm to me, and shows me lines carved there, fresh and bleeding – rough, painful wounds that he has scratched into himself. I resist, I don't want to read, no speech, no language. But at last I have to look, and it takes my mind a moment to arrange the letters into the first word I have seen in days.

RUN

And he opens his mouth, and I see the torn scrap of muscle where his tongue used to be. My song ends like a stab and I turn to run and Mrs Quinn is there with us, standing at the head of the cairn. No farmer's wife now, she is dressed in nature – around her neck, a string of strange fruits, like apricots or figs or mushrooms, but shrivelled and congealed with their own dark juice…

I have been running all night, but I am no closer to the cottage. I can get nearly to the gate, but this must be a dream, because the dawn comes up and still I run, and still I am no closer. The birds sing, and then they fall silent. I see Mrs Quinn come out of the cottage, a young man behind her. He waves her goodbye, and when she has gone he looks inside the sentry box, takes out a basket, a tartan flask inside it, food. I scream for him to stop, but no sound comes from the wound of my mouth.

He turns and walks back into the house. I will have to wait for night to fall.

Mad Maisy Sad

Suzy Ceulan Hughes

I have stayed too long in this place and it is full of ghosts. They jostle me on the pavement and in the narrow aisles of the village shop.

Sometimes I walk in there and know that Cai is around the corner, picking through the carrots and the apples. He will buy only two or three of each, leaving the rest marked with his scent. The rancid smell of unwashed hair and clothes, old cooking fat and body odour. The scent of loneliness and neglect.. How long has he been dead now…?

I put the bag of sugar, the apples – I hope they're not the ones Cai has touched, and I shall wash them when I get home, just in case – and the *Western Mail* on the counter.

'But Maisy,' says Gwen the Shop. 'That's the third bag of sugar you've bought today. Are you sure you want so much?'

'No, no,' I say. 'You must be mistaken. I just went to make myself a cup of tea and realised I'd forgotten the sugar when I came in earlier, and the newspaper and apples, too.'

'Ah well,' she says. 'If you're sure.'

And she taps the items into the till and packs them in my bag for me.

She's quite right, of course, that I have bought three bags of sugar today. But this time I'm being forgetful with intent. The sloes are ripe and ready for gin-making, but I hardly need the whole village to know I like a tipple. I've saved the bottles carefully from last year, and I bought the gin some weeks ago, on my last trip into town. There's enough gossiping goes on in this village without giving them cause for it. And I should know…

See dear Mari walking up the street there? She's round and grey now, her breasts sagging to her belly and her hair wisping over her ears. Her knees have gone and she walks with sticks, slowly. Ah, but she was a one. She had true blonde curls well into her forties, and fine breasts whose nipples pointed to the sky. Our men use to vie with each other for which of us had the best bottom in the village. All gone now, of course, the laughing men and the pert buttocks.

Mari thought life fun, and there were those who hated her for it. Time she grew up and acted her age, they'd say. Mutton dressed up as lamb. And they would purse their lips so tight they looked as though they were sucking wasps.

'I'd like a stamp as well,' I say, 'for my son's birthday card. It's his birthday on Thursday, you see, though I can't for the life of me remember how old he is.'

'But Maisy,' says Gwen, 'your son is dead. Have you forgotten that Peter died?'

I stare at her. I had forgotten, this morning, when I was writing the card: 'To dear Peter, with love always and forever from your mother.' But now she says it, I know she's right.

I look down at the envelope lying on the counter, and for a moment fail to recognise the cramped and shaken handwriting that is now mine. I wonder who is living at the address that once was his. What will they do with this card addressed to a man they've perhaps never heard of? He would be grey and almost old himself now, I think. If he hadn't died.

I look out of the window and see that Mari has stopped for a breather, resting those once-pert buttocks against Evan's low garden wall. I suddenly remember that Peter had a bit of a thing for Mari when he was a boy. She was beautiful, and kind as well. A teenager's perfect pin-up. What would he say if he could see her now I wonder? I know straight away that he'd be sad. It's Mari who's the ghost, I think, not Peter. Does that make me a ghost, too?

Gwen the Shop is waiting. I glance down at the envelope and then lift my head to look at her again, making sure my chin is tilted slightly upwards. I still have a fine nose to look down, if that's the way they want to see it.

'I should like a first-class stamp, if you please,' I say.

As I walk back down the street, I engage in light conversation with other ghosts. They're surprised, because usually I ignore them, brush aside their vacuous greetings. But today I am sociability itself. I do not want to think of Peter being dead. It isn't right, for a mother to outlive her son. It's nature all gone wrong.

'Auntie Maisy, are you all right?'

She's a mere slip of a thing. I have not the faintest idea

who she is. For a moment I am confused. I seek some resemblance in her face.

'I do not have a niece,' I say.

And then I remember. Of course, this is how it is. The young people call everyone Auntie and Uncle. She is somebody else's daughter or granddaughter or niece. Not mine. I refuse to remember that my lovely niece is also dead, even longer dead than Peter. How can it be? It isn't right.

You were my golden ones, the two of you. Let us leap the cracks between the paving stones, so the crocodiles can't nip our toes. Let us hold hands and dance along the twilight promenade, the adults smiling at our antics. Let us feel the still-warm sand beneath our feet as we dodge the waves.

See the dolphins leaping. See the starlings swoop beneath the pier. See the moon, hanging huge and yellow in the navy sky.

With you, I became a child again. How many years ago? You've both been gone so long now. Yet your presence here is stronger than mine, though I am still alive.

'I'm sorry, Maisy,' says the girl.

She is not at all abashed. Young people are so confident these days.

'I thought you were crying and wondered if you were all right.'

'I'm fine,' I say. 'It's this wretched wind getting in my eyes.'

I take my handkerchief from my pocket and wipe my cheeks, decorously, I think. She smiles at me. There is no wind, not the slightest hint of it.

'Would you like me to walk home with you?' she says. 'I could carry your bag, if you like.'

'That's very kind,' I say. 'But there's no need, really.'

When I reach the corner, though, the bag feels suddenly heavy in my hand. The lights are glowing in the window of the pub and I think I'll pop in, just for a while, to break my journey and see who's there.

It's difficult to reach the bar through the throng of ghosts in their familiar places. I don't want to be moithering Llew. Such a quiet and gentle man, who would yield his place without a word, even if I were unwittingly stepping on his toes. His elbows are on the bar, his pint in front of him. Yes, Llew was a gentleman. Not like Eddie, sitting on the tall stool in the corner, looking for all the world like a leprechaun. More mischief than malice, that one, but with the foulest mouth. Can't be worrying too much about him. He'll swear at me however wide a berth I give him. 'Stay your tongue, Eddie, there's a lady present.' 'Well, *Duw Duw*, bloody Saes…' You'd have thought he was Welsh himself, but there, that's another story.

When I've navigated the invisible presences at the bar, there will be the problem of where to sit. Never, never on the end of the settle at the corner of the bar opposite Eddie. For that was Dewi's place. And his is not a lap I'd want to be sitting on. Dear Dewi, a dewdrop forever hanging from the end of his spiky nose and occasionally falling – plip, plop – into the tepid beer he's been hugging to him for the past hour. Poor dab.

'I'd like a sherry,' I say. 'A large measure of Harvey's

Bristol Cream poured over ice into a tall, slim glass. I like a sherry at this time of year.'

I drink sherry only at Christmas. It goes with mince pies and pickled walnuts and other things you wouldn't think of having at any other time.

Oddly, the sherry is before me in a trice, as though the barman knew already what I should order, even though I'm making an exception and it isn't Christmas at all.

I thank him and carry my glass carefully towards the table in the bay window. I weave my way politely through the ghosts. They stand aside for me today, though they don't always. It depends who's there, of course. There's a space on the bench seat under the window, right in the middle. It's my favourite place. The ghosts tuck in their feet and swing their knees aside to let me in.

'Thank you,' I say. 'Thank you so much. I'm very grateful.'

They raise their glasses to me in a silent toast. I raise mine in return. It feels good to have their quiet company around me, to know they are all still here. I take a sip of sherry, and my heart feels warm and full.

'Happy Christmas, Maisy,' the barman calls to me across the empty room.

'Thank you,' I say. 'And the same to you.'

I know it is September, but I wouldn't wish to disillusion him.

A Soldier's Tale

Jacqueline Harrett

I stand alone by the railway track. This place is desolate, hushed as a deaf man's world. Even the birds have deserted. This is the end of the line but no trains come here now. The tracks are rusted, dirty brown where once they gleamed. No engines screech through the mist. No swirl of grey smoke into the pewter skies. That was in the beginning, but no longer. Days, weeks, years have passed. I have lost track of time. It no longer matters. Things were different then. I was a soldier of the Reich and this is my tale.

I joined up when I was sixteen. I was tall for my age so I lied and no-one checked or questioned too closely. It was all for the Fatherland. I was proud to wear my uniform and ignored my mother's tears and father's silence when I left. My little sister wept and asked who would help her to dig the potatoes or milk the cow and I laughed, full of the joy of going off to war. This was my freedom. I gave no thought to their grief only the glory to come. I was strong; I could run fast and shoot a rifle better than many of my friends. I was sure I would be posted to the front line and itched for the splendour of war. How foolish were those boyhood dreams. No glory for me. Instead I was sent here to be a guard at the camp.

'Easy job,' the commandant bellowed. 'They show any sign of insolence or disobedience then shoot. Dirty Jews.' He spat on the floor.

He was right. It was easy, at first. Trains rattled into the station, belched steam and disgorged their cargo. Men, women and children tumbled out of carriages, bewildered, blinking in the light. Silent. With them came the smell – fetid and ripe with fear. I ignored it all. I held my chin high and my gun higher – proud to be serving the Fatherland. They shuffled from the railway track into the camp where we took everything from them. I didn't think about it. I didn't see them as people but as animals, worse than animals. It was, after all, for the glory of the Fatherland.

Then, the girl came. Usually the Jews kept their eyes averted but she was different. She stepped from the train, filthy and ragged; her yellow star displayed clearly, her long brown hair loose around her shoulders. She stopped and stared at me until, aware of her scrutiny, I looked back. Her gaze was disdainful. She inspected me from head to toe and then back again, as if she was superior. She reminded me of my little sister. Then she stared right into my eyes. I recognised something in that look and felt shame creeping into my thoughts. I blushed, much to my annoyance. This was a war but were these creatures the enemy? How did killing them serve the Fatherland? For the first time I questioned the purpose of my task but I was a soldier, trained to obey. I did not dare to falter or question aloud.

My thoughts had to be kept secret, locked deep inside my head. I dared not acknowledge these doubts, even to myself. I was a soldier of the Reich but I could not avert my eyes from hers.

'Magda,' someone hissed and she turned her head and moved to join the others. The spell was broken. She was herded off to the women's compound although she was only a child, eleven or twelve perhaps.

After that Magda seemed to be everywhere I looked. Her hair was cut off and she wore the striped pyjamas of the camp but I would have known her anywhere. Her eyes seemed to follow me, reproaching, filling me with guilt. She was the same age as my little sister. She was hungry. They were all hungry. I started to think about what we were doing to these innocents. I could see my little sister's face and wondered how she would feel in this place.

We had supplies. We were fed and given rations, meagre enough but more than the Jews who faded into skeletons in front of us. Many died before they reached the gas chambers. I shall never know why Magda had an effect on me. It felt unnatural. Her eyes searched my innermost thoughts and formed some strange telepathy. It was unreal and made me restless in my sleep, sometimes waking in a sweat imagining Magda pointing at me. As the days went on I could almost feel her hunger so when I thought no one was watching I would drop some bread or other scraps near her. Magda never acknowledged the food and I was careful not to say anything in case someone spotted me. We never spoke.

As the weeks passed she grew thinner, gaunt and pale. Her eyes seemed to be too large for her face. The cold was biting and even the heavy uniform did not stop it seeping into my bones. I wondered how she survived. I was desperate to help her and in my desperation I became careless. I was caught about to pass bread through the wire to her. I knew I was in trouble when the commandant demanded to see me.

'Guterman,' the commandant almost whispered. He was at his most dangerous when he was controlled. I expected to be severely punished, beaten perhaps or even shot for fraternising with the enemy. I held my breath, wondering what was to follow.

'It seems Guterman, that you want to be closer to the filthy Jews. Is that right?' A spray of spit accompanied his question.

'Nein, Herr Commandant. It was an error. It won't happen again, sir.' My heart was beating so loudly it was rivalling the clock on the wall.

He smiled, showing a gap where he had lost a front tooth. 'I think Guterman, you need to see what happens to vermin. You are assigned to guard the chambers. You can take the little Jews to be gassed and see what happens to enemies of the Fatherland. Now, out, before I change my mind and have you thrown in there yourself.

'Heil Hitler!'

'Heil Hitler!'

I staggered out of the commandant's office, my head reeling. Relief at not being executed was mingled with horror. Guard duty at the chambers was something discussed in quarters. Some of the guards spoke little about it but their faces betrayed the strain, while others boasted about how many 'stinking Jews' had been exterminated. It reminded me of my father talking about rat-catching on the farm and keeping the pests under control. There were rumours about what happened to the bodies, and the smells of human flesh as they were processed were stronger close to the chambers. The air was often pungent with the smoke from the incinerators. Those days at the gas chamber were the worst of my life. I prayed every night to be taken to the front line to die with honour. There was no honour in this herding of the old and ill, women and children into the death pits. I closed my eyes, ears and mind to these horrors and had to remind myself daily that it was all for the glory of the Fatherland. Screams filled my sleep and the smells seeped into my uniform, which made eating difficult. I longed to be back in my home and the arms of my mother. I wanted to be a child again, before the war, before hatred had filled our country and before my innocence had been lost.

The day Magda went into the chamber was my last. She gazed at me with understanding and nodded slightly, almost smiling as she went to her death as quietly as she had lived her short life. Her courage and acceptance of her fate made me shake uncontrollably. The other guards looked at me with pity.

I lay awake all night, haunted by the sight of her as she walked almost with pride, and without fear, to her death. I had a vision of my little sister entering the gas chamber and shuddered. Realisation hit me. There was no glory in this game of soldiers. I thought of the shame of my father and the pain of my mother but I knew what I had to do. There was no other way, no other solution for my pain.

In the morning, I washed and dressed as usual. I brushed my uniform and polished my boots until they shone. I was no longer the naïve young boy of sixteen with idealistic thoughts of war. Two years had passed and I was a man and ready to act like a man of honour. I couldn't eat. The porridge felt like lumps of chalk in my mouth. I was sweating, despite the cold. Chin high, I marched to the central square, a soldier of the Reich. Trembling, I put my gun to my head.

I stand alone by the railway track, for all eternity.

The Pull of the North

Rona Laycock

Amelia hated the sound of the wind in the trees. The way it howled and buffeted its way through the copse at the back of their house. She would hear voices mingled with the clashing of branches; voices as old as the mountains that surrounded the town. At night in particular, she could make out the cries of ghosts and the deep rumbling bass notes of demons and she would shudder in her bed unable to sleep. No one else in the house was worried; Siôn would laugh at what he called her fantasy life and the twins just looked bewildered for a while if she mentioned it and then they would go back to their toys.

She loved the girls with every atom in her body but she couldn't understand them. To look at them you would think the only DNA they had inherited was from her but in their heads they were Siôn's. They only thought in concrete facts. Even from a young age they had had immense concentration when they played with building blocks and toy animals, but when she had tried to tell them tales from her homeland their attention would wander and she could see them staring longingly at their toys. Perhaps it was too much to ask; they couldn't imagine the golden shine of gelid water at sunset; the vivid blues found in calving glaciers or the white mountains of ice that sailed past brightly coloured settlements. She would tell them the stories her mother and grandmother had told her, about the souls that lived in everything: rocks, animals and plants. About how the human soul could move from animal to animal. And she would explain the morals of stories that showed how people should live their lives. They never questioned her about these tales, never asked for them to be told, they were happy to go to bed tired out after running around outside and she realised she was reciting the stories because of the fear that if she didn't keep telling them she would forget who she was.

When she had confided in Siôn's mother about the way the twins seemed not to be interested in stories, she had laughed. 'Just like Siôn,' she said. 'Never happier than when he could build up his bricks and knock them down or knock his brother's toys over.'

The first time Siôn hit her she wondered if she had imagined it. The blow was so sudden, so unexpected and his face so impassive as he lashed out. The twins had cried and rushed to her side and later she understood that that was why he had not hit her a second time that day. He lost his job at the boatyard because of a fight. She heard so many different stories; Siôn had started it, someone else had hit Siôn first, it had been a free for all, with fists and feet flying and Siôn just hit the wrong person – the foreman. Whatever the cause, Siôn had been fired on the spot and instead of coming home straightaway he had been in the Skull and Crossbones until the barman threw him out.

She was no stranger to alcohol, it was the scourge of her community back home; since the coming of the Danes and industry, many young Inuit men no longer learned the ways of their elders and they felt they had no role to play. They existed on handouts and occasional jobs in the tanneries and fish packing factories. Drink had become a solace and a curse; she had lost her youngest brother to alcohol. She remembered the night he didn't come home and the days spent searching for him, praying he would be found crashed out at a friend's place or in a boat. A week later he had been found, washed up amongst the debris on the fishing island. His body was tangled up in nylon netting and the verdict had been that he had stumbled into the harbour while he was drunk. It was not an uncommon story.

Siôn drank more and in his befuddled stupor he would blame her for being a millstone round his neck; there was nothing she could do as night after night he would sit in front of the television drinking whatever he could get his hands on. The twins were spared most of it as she made sure they were in bed long before he became abusive, although she knew he would never hurt them; even at his most drunken she could see he loved them and would be tender towards them. She just didn't want them to see what he did to her.

One night she had a dream that was so vivid it spilled over into her waking life. She was in the small church where they had got married. A tiny corrugated iron building that was dull green on the outside, but on the inside was painted a pure, beautiful white. Colour came from the abundance of wild flowers covering the altar, a gold cross that gleamed in the weak sunlight and the model ship that hung above the aisle. She was dressed in beaded skins, the traditional costume she had worn for the wedding and she could hear her mother singing – not hymns but an Inuit song of celebration. She opened her eyes but could still hear the music; as she prepared breakfast for the girls her head filled with visions and sounds from her village to the south of Qaqortoq. There was a letter from home on the doormat, she tucked it unopened into her pocket; she needed somewhere quiet to read it.

After walking the girls to school, she went to the tiny church of St Philip that was perched halfway up the mountain. Unlike the big parish church in town, this church was intimate in scale and she felt safe within its granite walls.

Winter was coming, she could feel it in the whispers borne on the north wind; soon it would snow and the mountains would sparkle in bright cold sunlight and she would feel the tug of home. It happened every year.

She pulled the letter out of her coat pocket and looked at the writing on the envelope. Not her mother's; she ripped it open and saw that it was from her uncle. Everything she had dreaded was in the letter; her mother had died. Suddenly and without warning. She tried to make sense of the words – aneurysm, very fast, didn't suffer. What did any of that matter?

She walked back to her house in despair. The day passed

and the children came home; she made their tea and helped them with their homework. Their voices were strange, the language was wrong, their laughter was wrong; she watched them as they built bridges and houses with brightly coloured bricks. Left to their own devices they would build for hours. They built towns and cities that were completely alien to her. Siôn came in in high spirits; he had found a job on the ferries – good pay. He threw himself down beside the girls and they built and built; the living room filled with a miniature city of hard edged shopping centres, office blocks and flats. Here and there the girls placed plastic trees but nothing interrupted the regimented streets and blocks. There was nothing organic in their project, nothing Amelia could identify with.

The girls went happily to bed; no time for stories, they were too tired. Amelia kept her hand on the letter as she listened to Siôn talk about the good times that were coming. They went to bed and for the first time in ages they made love.

At midnight Amelia felt her mother call; she got up and went to the window. The sky was clear and the stars shone with a brittle light. She went into the girls' room, bent over them and whispered their Inuit names in their ears so that they would never forget who they were, then she pulled sealskin mukluks on over thick socks and dressed in her fur anorak. She had not worn it since arriving in Wales. She listened; all was silent in the house as she let herself out of the front door.

In darkness she walked to the path that led to the little

church on the mountain and climbed up the steep incline. It was silent and very cold; her breath came in sobs as she passed the church and pushed on up the mountainside. Clouds were gathering above her and the stars were fading and being covered. When she reached the summit she stopped and looked down over the town; streetlights shone yellow and she could just make out some of the houses, but not her own. She climbed over the summit and found a small cwm in the lee of some rocks where she sat down. She watched the last of the stars being smothered by the clouds and then snowflakes started to fall. She took off her anorak, folded it and placed it under her head as she lay down. The cold was welcome and the snow did its best to envelop her as she fell asleep to the sounds of her mother singing.

Seashells

Gillian Drake

Lowri eased the car along the Pembrokeshire lane. The sky was leaden, overcast and misty, and the grey line of the sea was barely visible on the horizon. A tangle of wild flowers fringed the road – pretty on a sunny day, she thought, but today the daisies were tightly closed and the wild roses hung their heads, heavy with rain.

She glanced at the estate agent's details on the seat beside her. Shell Cottage. She would surely be there soon. It was a pity Sam had been unable to take time off work so that they could view the house together. But, 'A house like that won't be on the market long,' he had said. 'It'll be another fortnight before I've finished this account and it could be gone by then. You go; you can let me know what you think.'

She sighed as yet another bend in the road appeared before her. This place was so remote…she feared that she already knew what she thought of it. True, the cottage looked delightful in the property details, but then it was the estate agent's job to make sure that it did. Moving to Pembrokeshire for Sam's job transfer sounded fine in theory, but what would it be like to live in an old, probably damp, cottage after their comfortable flat in Cardiff Bay? In the two years since they married she had settled happily there, enjoying being able to walk through town to her job in the small mail-order business that had now folded, leaving her redundant. How would she adjust to life in the country – especially in weather like this? Perhaps they would be better off looking for something in the town of Haverfordwest after all.

Her phone rang. There was no other traffic in the lane and Lowri stopped the car in a lay-by.

'Are you there yet?' Sam's cheerful voice was so welcome.

'Couple of miles to go,' said Lowri.

'How's it looking? Promising?'

'Can't really tell…' She peered into the drizzle. Fields, a wood in the distance, the rooftops of what must be the village, huddled below a church tower. 'Be better when the mist clears.' She hoped with all her heart that it really would.

'I'll ring you in about an hour, then.' She heard the sound of a phone in the background, busy voices. 'I'll have to go,' he added. 'Sorry!'

Lowri drove the last mile or two, arriving at Shell Cottage as arranged at three o'clock. As the sound of the engine died down into the silence, she formed her first impression of the place. 'Tucked into a fold of the hillside, on the edge of the village on the road to the sea…' well, the estate agent had been right about the location. She got out of the car and swung open the wooden gate with its peeling blue paint. The path to the front door was of shingle: stones and small pebbles, mixed with masses of tiny shells. Along its length was a border of larger shells – cockles, scallops, even the occasional big nautilus, interspersed with smaller whelks, limpets, cowries and mussels. It wasn't difficult to see how the cottage had got its name. Somebody must have collected these for years, adding them to the border and also to the tops of the low walls which surrounded the house.

Lowri approached the front door. In the flowerbeds, Canterbury bells, lavender, foxgloves, stocks, crowded together in front of a wild rose hedge, mixed with bindweed and, she noticed, plenty of dandelions. An elderly lady had lived all her life in the house, the estate agent had told her on the phone; she had passed away peacefully in the local hospital. Now, there was only a nephew in Australia who could not come back to take possession of it. The place looked a bit neglected, but then it had been empty for some time.

As arranged, the key was in the lock. That would never happen in Cardiff – or almost anywhere else, for that matter.

Lowri pushed the door, surprised to find that it opened easily. The house had charm, certainly, she thought, looking at the windows set deeply into the thick walls, the upstairs dormers protruding like raised eyebrows over the roof edge. But it would need a lot of work. Nothing had been changed here for years, by the look of it. She felt rather daunted at the prospect. DIY was hardly Sam's speciality, but he would cheerfully set to and get started, she knew; and besides, he had wanted to get away from what he called the 'Rat Race' for some time now.

The door led to a narrow passageway with old terracotta floor tiles underfoot. There were two rooms, one on either side of the passageway, and at the end, an antiquated kitchen with a stone butler's sink and some huge wooden cupboards, which must have been there since the house was built. No other furniture remained anywhere in the house; nothing to indicate the tastes of the woman who had lived there for so many years. Lowri turned back and set off upstairs to the bedrooms. No central heating either, she noted drily, folding her arms and wishing she had brought her jacket in with her.

What should she tell Sam? There was work to be done, certainly, but more importantly, would they be happy here? Uncertainty overwhelmed her as she plodded up the stairs, her footsteps echoing on the wooden treads.

At the top of the stairs there was a bathroom with a claw-footed bath, and then, across the landing, three bedrooms with deep set windows at knee level and uneven floors. As she entered the smallest of these, she stopped suddenly. This room, like all the others, was empty but on one wall was a picture: painting, print, photograph…? It was difficult to tell. Whoever had cleared the house had obviously overlooked it. Lowri crossed the creaking floorboards for a closer look. The picture showed a young girl aged about eight standing on the sea shore. She wore a faded floral dress and a battered straw hat, and was absorbed in gazing into a rock pool. Her long hair fell over her face and she held up the hem of her dress delicately in both hands, to make a sort of hammock for the seashells she was collecting.

Lowri was captivated. She glanced around the neat room at the wallpaper patterned with seaside flowers and shells. A small wardrobe and low-level chest of drawers had been built in on either of the cast-iron fireplace: the room must have belonged to a child. Perhaps it had been the bedroom of the owner of the house, when she was young. And maybe this was her on the wall. Lowri looked more closely at the picture, noticing that it was perfectly placed to catch the light from the single window: a window, she noticed, which framed a square of sky now surprisingly, gratifyingly, beginning to lighten from dull, heavy pewter to soft, pale grey.

Lowri went downstairs and flung open the back door. A fresh breeze rushed in, swirling around the kitchen and stirring the old blue curtains that still hung at the window. Outside there was a wild garden divided by another shingle path edged with shells, leading straight to the beach. She caught the tang of the salt sea air, heard the cry of the gulls and the sound of the waves. A short walk followed by a scramble over some rocks soon brought her to a crescent-shaped sandy beach edged by low grassy cliffs. Pink sea thrift and glossy buttercups bobbed in the gentle breeze. Directly in front of the cliffs were rock pools. Lowri blinked. She had thought she was alone on the beach, but had caught sight of a sudden movement. She rounded a small promontory and saw a child, a girl of about eight years old. The child was gazing into one of the pools, completely absorbed in collecting shells. These she held in the hem of her trailing floral dress. Her face was obscured by long hair and a battered straw hat.

For a second, time seemed to stand still as a cloud moved over, and then the sun came out and illuminated the scene. The girl turned slowly, looked in Lowri's direction, and smiled. Then she waved. Lowri's heart lifted and she looked around in surprise, seeking perhaps the girl's parent, friends...but the beach was deserted and when she turned back to wave, the girl was gone.

Walking back, the sunlight was bright enough to make the raindrops sparkle on the grassy edge of the shingle path. It gleamed on the shells, highlighting their ribbed and whorled shapes and bringing out their delicate pinks and greys and soft beige colours, all glistening and shining with rain. The upstairs windows of the house flashed with gold, and the wet slate roof had turned to silver.

With a light step Lowri hurried back along the shell-lined path to the open door of the cottage. From there she stopped to look at the view before her, then reached for her phone and keyed Sam's number.

'Sam!' she cried, as his cheerful voice answered. 'The cottage! It's wonderful! We're home!'

Convention is the Mother of Reality or A Day in the Life of Alexandra Preston

Nic Herriot

'Oi, is that what you want to call it? Wasn't it Aleksandr Solzhenitsyn who was in the gulag in Siberia? You don't think you're in a Russian prison do you?'

'No, but I'm being made to do this aren't I?'

'Are you? I thought you liked these life story sessions?'

'Well... It was either this or the *art* class, colouring in between the lines of children's pictures.'

'Yes...well... She was misguided.'

'Where is she now anyway, have you guided her out the door yet?'

'Ooo, good one, now stop laughing, the laptop is on and ready to go, so where do you want to start?'

'Where I always start, with a cup of tea...'

*

'Morning, Alex, are you awake, would you like a cup of tea?'

'Oh hello, a cup of tea? Thank you.'

'A smile, cup of tea and breakfast when you're up and ready.'

I sit up slowly getting my bearings; I recognise the woman bringing my tea but can't remember her name. It feels too early in the morning. I feel that I'm on the wrong side of the bed, I never sleep on this side of the bed…and on my own, and where's Martha gone, why didn't she wake me?

'Has Martha gone already? Where is she?'

'I don't know love; she's probably at work and will come and see you this afternoon. Here's your cup of tea, I'll put it here on the table and leave you to wake up properly. Give me a bell if you need anything else before you get up.'

An old lady wanders in singing at the top of her voice. 'Onward Christian soldiers, marching as to war…'

Here we go again I think as she sings on. A verse into it someone shouts out, 'Pass the ammunition.' We all laugh, the old lady not noticing the kerfuffle continues her singing.

Martha joins me in time for tea break. I pass her a plate and cup and saucer. 'Have we had breakfast?'

'Yes, you had breakfast a few hours ago, you had a bacon sandwich, don't you remember?' The lady bringing me a cup of tea and biscuits answers before Martha can.

'Did I have tomato sauce on it?' I ask.

'Yes, you did cos I had to go down to the kitchen to ask for another bottle, we had run out.'

'I don't remember,' I whisper to Martha, 'but I do like tomato sauce on bacon sandwiches so she must be right.' I sort out the cups and plates of biscuits so she can reach them. 'Do you remember First Out, that little café we would go to when we arrived in London, before doing anything else? Lovely place, very friendly, shame it had to close down. A mug of tea and then walk down that long bookshop road, what was it called? To the woman's bookshop, Silver Moon. That's gone as well.' I play with my cup, thinking back, the tea too hot to drink.

That wasn't with me that was with your ex.

'Oh sorry, it's all one memory these days, but you have been there with me though haven't you?'

Yes, a couple of times.

'So it wasn't with you I went to that club, Vixens, when I finally knew I was in the right place?'

No, that was her again, but I don't mind, if you didn't go to that club you would never have been with me.

I squeeze Martha's hand. 'I would have, in the end, eventually, like *Sliding Rooms*, we always get to where we are going in the end.'

Doors, the film was called *Sliding Doors*.

I absentmindedly lift off the top layer of my bourbon biscuit, triumphant in the fact that it comes off leaving the chocolate filling intact.

'Can Charlotte join you?' I look up from my dislocated biscuit and use it to point to the spare chair so Lottie can join us. I rearrange our cups and plates around to make room for her.

'Morning Lottie, I haven't seen you for ages.'

I turn to Martha. 'We met at the library, didn't we Lottie, we go there together now cos we both like to read.'

'And the quiet. I like to read the books and the wassanames. Those and then we do the, the thing.' Lottie turns imaginary pages with her hands, describing the magazines we read.

A couple walk up to our table. They are holding hands. 'We would like to book a taxi to Aberystwyth and two hotel rooms please.'

I look at Martha and Lottie confused. 'We are in Aberystwyth aren't we?' I ask.

'Oh, thank you,' replies the man. 'Can we see our hotel rooms please?'

The tea lady comes up. 'Can I help? Can I show you your rooms, they are this way…'

'Thank you, shall we pay for them now?' They walk away with the tea lady to see their rooms.

'Isn't he, you know, wassa…wassaname, got a thingy?' Lottie points to the rings on her hand.

'I don't think that's his wife, is it?' I know I've got a bad memory but…'

The tea lady comes back and sits at our table.

'Yes, and I hope he has forgotten about his weekend away when his wife comes to visit this afternoon.'

Lottie giggles. 'There's going to be trouble.'

'There's a call for you, on your iPad, it's your son, and do you want to chat to him?'

I'm handed a picture of someone waving at me.

'Hello, Mum.'

'Is that you, Dad? What're you doing calling me here?'

'No, Mum, it's Simon, your son, Granddad is…'

Martha nudges me up to sit next to me on the sofa. I turn the photo frame slightly so she can see.

That's Simon, silly, can't you tell?

'We thought you would like to see your brand new great-grandson. He's only three days old.'

The picture swings about as Simon moves his iPad towards a girl waving madly and holding a baby.

'Oh look, it's…it's…'

It's Rachel, your granddaughter. As usual Martha steps in to give me a name I've forgotten for a face that is not forgotten.

I peer at the screen. 'He's lovely, and very small.'

He's only three days old. She tells me.

A boy appears next to Rachel. 'Hello Granny Preston. What do you think? Isn't he lovely? We haven't got a name yet; we are trying out various ones to see what fits him.'

The images blur as it's moved. Simon appears again. 'Mum, I'm coming over to visit next week so I'll bring some photos for you.'

'We could go out and get a little present for him.' I turn to the lady standing near-by. 'Where is my money kept? Do I have any?'

'Yes, your money is kept in the office, it's safe. You can get it if you want to go shopping.'

'There you go, Simon. We'll go shopping and get something for him.'

'OK, Mum, see you next week, I'll give you a last look at the little fellow before I sign off. Bye.'

I wave at Rachel and her little baby and the other man who is waving back and their faces disappear.

'Is this yours?' I ask as I hold up the photo frame to the lady who has stood up. 'Yes, I'll put it safe up here for next time you need it. He looks a lovely little baby.'

'Yes, he's my grandson,' I say proudly.

'Great-grandson.' Say the lady and Martha at the same time. 'I'm not old enough to be a great-granny,' I laugh. 'I don't feel that old anyway.'

'It's lunchtime now, do you want to come along for some lunch?' Someone comes up to us. I squint at her badge. *Kathy.*

'I haven't cooked anything? How have I managed to make lunch when I've been with Lottie?'

'When you paid for your room all your food was included, so all your meals get cooked for you. Like if you were staying in a hotel or something.'

'Oooooo, there's posh. I get fed-up with cooking all the time so I'm glad it's not me today. Imagine cooking for this lot.' I point to some people sitting by the window. I smile at her and take her proffered arm as she walks me to my table.

Martha appears on my other side. You are such a flirt; I saw that, you smiling at Kathy. A big grin on her face, knowing she has caught me out.

'I don't know what you mean, and anyway I have three words to say to you, York – Festival – Rona Cameron.'

That's four words.

'I have four words to say…'

Whisht now. Martha squeezes my hand, you do go on. I smile in return and take my time to rearrange the table so there is room for her. Lottie sits on my other side. 'Hello Lottie, are you having lunch with us? You're in luck, I didn't cook this. Apparently we have staff who cook for us.'

'Yes, I know…sometimes they do it in the you know…' She makes a stirring motion with her hands.

'We always have lunch cooked for us.' A big booming voice comes out across the dining room.

'Shut up,' shouts someone from another table.

We lean in together, and laugh. 'Here we go,' giggles Lottie, 'Going to be trouble in the, you know, what'saname.'

I sit on the sofa dozing. A lady sits down beside me.

'She's nuts, she shouldn't be here.' She points her finger at the lady sitting at a table, using her other hand to hide the fact that she is pointing to her.

'What did she say?' the marked out lady asks me.

'She is asking what time lunch is.' I reply, one eye squinting at the woman who woke me up.

'What did she say?' the first lady points at her again.

I get up and go and find Martha. There is going to be trouble in here and I want nothing of it.

Someone I recognise comes up to me, smiling.

'How do you fancy going shopping this afternoon, I thought you might like to buy some new shirts.' It's Emma who is holding a taxi's card, phone in her other hand.

'Do I have any money to buy things; I haven't got any on me.'

'Don't worry I have your card here; it's kept in the office so it doesn't get lost.'

'Are you going to carry it for me then, in case I lose it?'

'Yes, I can keep it in my pocket. We're going with Charlotte and Zoe.'

'Can Martha come? Is there room in the car for her?' I look around for Martha not even sure where she is but not wanting to leave her behind.

'I'm sure Martha can find her own way there if you tell her where we are going.'

'Where are we going again?'

'We're going to the shopping centre; I thought you would like to see what they have there.'

'Will you be able to find it?' I ask Martha. She kisses my cheek. I'll be there.

I snuggle down into my coat; it's my favourite, it reminds me of my duvet.

'I love this coat,' I zip it up and pull the collar up around my ears. 'It's like wearing a duvet, like being in bed.'

'It looks warm and you'll need it, it's cold out today.'

Lottie is rummaging through her handbag and looks up. 'It's a lazy…you know…blows all round you.'

'Wind? Do you mean wind? What's a lazy wind?' asks Emma.

'It's what my mum used to say. A wind that goes through you, it's too lazy to go round you.' Lottie is still searching through her handbag. She pulls out a spare jumper, a dog bowl and some biscuits and a hairbrush and then stuffs them back in.

I peer in. 'You've got everything in there. What do you want a dog's bowl for?'

'It's for…for…the whatshername, you know, the brown thing.'

'The dog?'

'Yes, the dog, we've got a dog across the hall. Need to have you know…the things.'

'Have we got everyone now?' asks Emma.

'We haven't got a dog though, I know that much.' I mutter to Martha. Whisht now, that's not like you. Why can't she have a dog…?

We leave the warmth of the hallway to get into the taxi.

Lottie looks up at the clouds, 'The sky's all mouldy.'

'Mouldy?' queries Emma, looking up. 'Yes, I guess that's a good word for it, might even snow.'

'Wow, it is huge. So much stuff.'

Emma goes off with Lottie who has gone to look at the shoes.

I reach out to the first rail of bright flowery shirts and as I touch a shirt, it falls onto the floor. I pick it up and put it back on the rail but it misses and falls down again. I knock the next one off trying to pick it up. Zoe comes to my rescue and as I move out of her way Martha walks towards me. I watch her and smile, remembering that very first time in that nightclub she walked towards me.

I put my arms out encompassing the store. 'Have you ever seen so much stuff? Look at the shirts, aren't they wonderful?'

And bright. Martha puts her arm through mine, bringing us closer.

'Would you like to try one of these on?' Zoe is holding up two shirts.

'Can I? Which one do I want? Can I have both?'

I have a basketful of shirts and I watch a television screen showing me lots of furniture and people sitting on sofas. Martha has wandered off again, probably to look at the kitchen things.

I walk into the sitting room, showing off my new shirt. 'Very lovely,' says the lady from lunch time.

'Too loud,' shouts the man who looks up from watching the TV, and who is always too loud.

'How can my shirt be louder than you? This is the height of fashion.' I shout back, at the same time as doing a twirl to a lady applauding me.

'Richard, leave the telly alone now and come and have your tea, come and sit over here.'

'Not near me, I don't want him sitting at our table.'

'No, he can sit here, you sit at that table with Sally and Lottie, and at least they are not causing trouble.' She gives me a wink and I settle down. I look to see where Martha will sit. I sort out her knife, fork and spoon, making sure she can sit next to me.

'I hope it's not spaghetti bolognese,' I say. 'I always make a mess when I wear new shirts and eat spaghetti.'

'It's so bright no one will notice. Did you get free sunglasses with it? Anyway, it's chicken curry. You might be safer with this.' Carol puts my tea in front of me. 'Who's the other place set for? You expecting guests?'

'Do you remember as a kid wanting to sleep in your Brownie uniform?'

'What?' I look at Sally.

'When I got my first Brownie uniform, I didn't want to take it off, I was so proud I wanted to sleep in it. Mum wouldn't let me. Said I had to hang it up, keep it special. The next morning she came in and found me with it on under my pyjamas.'

'Welly boots. I loved my red wellies when I was little; I wanted to wear them in the wassa…wassaname, when Mum wanted to…me.' Lottie mimes washing her face. 'I wanted to wear them to school. She said, "no."'

'My daughter wouldn't take off her new ninja warriors t-shirt when she got one for Christmas last year.' Carol came over with another plate of curry. 'Wore it till it could walk by itself. I had to pinch it off her and wash it one night. Here you go, Sally, if you were a Brownie are you prepared for this curry?'

'Always.' Sally holds up a spoon ready to eat.

'What did you want to wear and never take off?' Carol asks me as she serves Lottie.

'I dunno really, I was too young to remember…maybe I didn't wear any clothes.'

'I'm not having people with no clothes on in here.' Richard shouts from the other table.

'Shut up listening,' shouts back Sally.

I grin at Lottie who giggles. 'Going to be trouble in the, the…'

In my favourite blue pyjamas I get into bed and watch Carol put a mug of tea on my bedside table.

'This is very small for a double bed isn't it?' I ask.

'It's a single bed. Why would you want a bigger one?'

'I like a bit of room to move about, though. I like a bit of leg room.'

'I didn't think you were that big.' She laughs. 'See you tomorrow.' She waves goodnight as she leaves.

Martha settles in next to me. I put my book down and snuggle down next to her.

You didn't tell the writer about the woman with the yellow buckets in her shed.

'I know, apparently I was running out of word count. I'll tell her the next time she comes. Now shove over a bit, I've hardly got any bed.'

Yeah, but you've got all the duvet.

'Remember how we laughed at the double beds we slept in on holiday? God, they were huge. You used to say we needed to be tied together with a rope or you'd lose me in them.'

Night night, she says, love you. I reply by putting my arm around her, tucking in close. 'Am I on the wrong side of the bed again?'

You are never on the wrong side of my bed.

'Martha!'

Whisht, I'm asleep. What?

'It was meant to be a ghost story; I didn't get around to telling the woman about her either.'

Ghosts

Pam Clatworthy

'That's it then.' Tom the general handyman locked the door of the empty tearoom and handed the key to Kezzie. He looked around the Tudor knot garden, there was not a soul in sight.

'Seems strange to see no one here.'

Kezzie picked up the last remnant of litter, a salt and vinegar crisp packet, and fumbled in her overall pocket.

'I nearly forgot this, Tom, your share of the tips. Mrs. Proctor sorted it out last night. The visitors have been really generous this year and we've had so many of them, all due to the *Haunted Houses and Gardens* series on TV, I suppose. Surprising what a bit of ghostly publicity can do. The "most haunted country cottage in Wales" certainly brought them in. We should do even better next year.'

Tom looked at her.

'I don't really believe in ghosts, but lots of the visitors said they'd seen something. Are you sure you're going to be all right here alone until we open again next Easter?'

Kezzie laughed. 'We've only funny, quirky spirits haunting us here, they never speak or shriek or groan and they do nothing harmful. I'll be fine, Tom, thanks. Now off you go and have a bit of fun before going back to college.

You deserve it. See you next year, I hope, and thanks for all your help this summer, you've been so good with even the most difficult of old dears.'

The late autumn sun was blazing red behind low western clouds when Kezzie finally threw her boots in the corner of the kitchen and filled up the kettle to make tea. The water pipes grumbled as usual and loud cracking noises in ancient woodwork filled the room as the pipes expanded. Out of the corner of her eye Kezzie fancied she spotted a pale wraith making for the door.

'Come back Mabel, please don't get so upset,' she pleaded. 'I'm only making myself a cup of tea. I've told you over and over again, Mr. Bartlett has gone forever. He's been dead for nearly two hundred years now. I know he was a bad master and because you murdered his prize bloodhound by feeding it rat poison, he threw you down the well. I can understand your fear of water it must have been awful for you, but please let bygones be bygones so that I can have my tea in peace.'

Kezzie's plea seemed to do the trick. Mabel hovered around a few minutes more before disappearing into the wall. The sudden loud scratching at the ancient door that led from the kitchen into courtyard was no surprise to Kezzie and always made her smile. For whenever Mabel disappeared, Rufus the red hound was always anxious to manifest himself.

'Come in, Rufus. She's gone so you need have no fear of being poisoned tonight.'

A large bloodhound moved towards Kezzie. The dog's

transparent body stood in front of the old green Aga, his white ribs superimposed over an oven door. Kezzie thought she could feel the draught from the animal's whisking tail, he was so real to her. She put out her hand and tentatively stroked where she imagined the dog's high domed head would be.

'You are a superior ghost,' she crooned to the nearly non-existent beast. 'A perfect pet. No barking, no drooling and no need for exercise. I'll miss you when I go skiing over Christmas, but I promise to come back as soon as I can.'

The dog sat obediently at Kezzie's command, then stretched out in front of the fireplace where he fell fast asleep, his body absorbing the dusty colours of the old rag rug. There were only three more ghostly inhabitants to go after the dog appeared. Kezzie knew that two of them would manifest themselves as soon as she turned the television set on and right on cue they appeared, standing behind her as she stretched out on the overstuffed chintz-covered sofa.

'Good evening gentlemen. I'm watching *The Adventures of Robin Hood* tonight,' she said, knowing how much they enjoyed that particular adventure story. 'Please sit down and join me in the viewing.'

She was always careful to speak in the most courteous manner to the old gentlemen who were used to the formality of mediaeval court life.

There was a flurry of excitement as the two burly Knights Templar pushed their way to sit down next to her, they did enjoy watching television. She moved over a little to give them room.

Kezzie had no fear of any of the strange spirits that thronged the house. Harmless creatures all. Even the two Crusaders had been peacefully sleeping in what was the old hunting lodge when a midwinter gale had brought the heavy, oak-beamed roof down on top of them. They had been on their way to the Second Crusade when tragedy struck and had been previously been shriven by the local priest before they left home, so they had both died a holy and sinless death. Now, the two sat peacefully and silently together holding hands, enjoying the cut and thrust of life in Sherwood Forest. Kezzie thought it shame they couldn't enjoy the chocolate that she would have been quite willing to share. Being well trained in good manners and chivalry they departed as soon as the final credits appeared on the screen, walking up a non-existent flight of stairs which had been removed during alterations in Victorian times.

At eleven o'clock, she made herself a bedtime drink. The old water pipes thrummed and as Mabel scooted around the kitchen in a frenzy of demented activity, Rufus made his departure through the locked door, not wishing to be re-poisoned by the simple creature, even though his death had been due to a mistaken use of the arsenic bottle in place of the worming cure, caused by misreading.

Kezzie's bedroom was under the eaves, it was warm and airless tonight. She flung open the casement window and as she leaned out to see if she could catch a glimpse of the sickle moon, she breathed in the sweet scent of the Albertine roses that flopped against the gnarled, split oak, window frame. They were truly the last roses of summer –

a sudden frost would kill them soon, beautiful ephemeral flowers with such a short lifespan. Unless, she thought, they too would reappear as ghostly ephemera once the old house was left to sleep and all humans had departed for the winter. It was a strange thought and Kezzie shivered for a second. Perhaps taking all the ghosts for granted was making her a strange creature. Indeed, the thought that she might be a ghost herself came into her mind but she shrugged it off. Would a ghost be capable of managing a haunted house, dealing with staff wages and tax returns? Not in a million years. Suddenly, a firm hand around her waist told her that the last and most joyous ghost of the evening had appeared in her room. A tall man stood beside her. He said nothing but he smiled and kissed her neck. She did not know who he was, where he came from or if he really was a ghost. She really didn't care. There was no explanation for his appearance; he had turned up one night in early Spring and had come again every night since. They never spoke, she never asked him questions. They just enjoyed each other. She turned to greet her lover and smiled at him, holding him close. His young, naked body felt warm to her touch and she knew that this was going to be the most perfect night in the most haunted cottage in Britain.

The Girl in the Grass

Caroline Clark

Emmie-May stood eye-deep in the ocean of grass. From above, her hair was only a patch of sunlight on its waves. Far out she watched two riders ploughing and leaping like dolphins. Their horses shouldered through, urged on by the riders' desperation, but plunging wildly in an effort to see their way. To Emmie-May they seemed haloed in a golden mist of pollen and midges wherever they broke the surface. The leading horseman passed; his red shirt was dark with sweat between the shoulders. He urged his mount forward without pause but his companion sometimes turned to stare along their wake. Emmie-May saw her white face whipped by her dark, braided hair, saw the tautness of her arms as she struggled to keep up.

Emmie-May moved towards the line of churned grass so that her figure appeared in the gap almost under the hooves of a third horseman whose tall, foam-flecked mount reared up and lunged sideways. He hauled it back, cursing then calming the beast. His weathered, work-seamed hands mastered it with skill, not brutal strength. He leaned down to peer at this sudden, impossible child.

Her coarse woollen dress was slicked with dew and grass-seeds, her fine blonde hair drifted like spider-silk around her. She showed no fear of the panicking horse or of his own fury but said, in a tone more puzzled than plaintive, 'My Mom won't wake up.'

'What in Hell are you doing out here, kid?'

The man's head jerked up as sounds of his quarry carried to him but the child's need compelled him.

'We live here. Grandpa's house is over there.' She pointed across apparently unbroken waves of green. 'But he died in the winter, and now Mom's just lying there, and I'm hungry…'

Jo Masterman cursed again, pushed his hat back off his brow to reveal wiry, greying hair as he wiped the sweat out of his eyes. The horse danced side-ways, sensing its rider's turmoil.

'Show me. Quickly. You can't have come far.'

He swung her up onto his thigh; there was no weight to speak of. He urged his horse in the direction she indicated and there, indeed, in a hidden dip, was the roof-ridge of a cabin.

Before he rode down Masterman cast one more fierce glance along the fading track of the fugitives. He looked across to the distant line of posts marking the railroad, then the three of them sank down into a pool of warm silence. As they approached the gateway all their horizon was shining grass.

Jo hitched his horse to the bleached rail and lifted Emmie-May down. She ran ahead of him, pushing the door open. It was an old, patched but not neglected place: bright rag-rugs on the board floor, blue and white china on the dresser. There was an old treadle sewing machine near the window where someone had been hemming a cotton frock. It lay, still tethered, in a flowery heap on a chair.

The child pulled him towards the inner doorway. There, like another abandoned dress, a white tangle of linen lay at the foot of a ladder. As his eyes adjusted to shadow, Jo saw a pale, closed face. He knelt and raised her head. Black blood, long dry, matted the ash-blonde hair. She was rigid and cold as the scrubbed floor.

'She's dead, like Grandpa, isn't she?' Emmie-May regarded him solemnly.

'Yes. I guess she fell – sleepwalked, maybe. I'll just take a look upstairs.'

Jo swung himself onto the ladder, taking care not to touch the woman below. Above, in the roof-space, was first a bunk-bed, tidily settled. The face of a small cloth doll smiled from the pillow. Beyond, a double bed lay open, its pieced quilt tumbled on the floor. An old-fashioned dress was draped across a chair, hairpins scattered on the table where a freckled mirror returned his ghostly image. An ordinary, lonely life had just stopped here – leaving a child marooned.

He heard a strange tinkling tune from below, picked up the quilt and, after a moment's thought, the doll. Then he swung back down the ladder. He covered the body, then went through to the living room where Emmie-May was curled on the rug. She was turning the handle of a small musical box from which came in uneven waltz-time, the *Streets of Laredo*.

'Have you got any folks in town?'

She shook her head. 'I been to church there though. That's where Grandpa is.'

Probably the Pastor would know about her. He could take it from there. Jo said, 'I'll take you over. Get a drink and a bite, then we'll go. Do you want this?'

He offered the smiling doll. Emmie-May hesitated then nodded and hugged it tight. The urgency seemed to have died out of him. He ladled a drink out of a half-full pail in the scullery and filled his canteen. The child finished a hunk of bread and stuffed another in her pocket. He wondered whether to ask if she wanted to say 'goodbye' to Mom but she trotted out of the door and he thought, 'Better not'.

Jo latched the door after them, he'd checked the back already. 'Ain't no dog here, anywhere?'

She shook her head. He lifted her up in front of him and roused the horse to take them from the close silence of the homestead up onto the whispering plain.

The only landmark was the railroad and he headed straight for the nearest point. He tied his neck-cloth to a post and laid stones in a rough arrow pointing along their track from the house, then he followed the rail-track towards the nearest town. He looked back once but the billowing grass showed only currents of the wind. For a while the girl hummed sleepily then, out of the blue, she asked, 'Why were you chasing them?'

Jo had been pre-occupied with thoughts of her future and was jolted back to his own concerns, which, an hour ago, had so obsessed him.

'My daughter,' he said. 'She just took off with a guy that's... Well, he's no good for her. Good enough stockman but...' his words ran into sand. He could not feel or even understand his own fury.

'She was scared. She was real scared. Were you goin' to whap her? Grandpa Andersen said he'd whap me once – when I took his good knife and dropped it down the well – but Mom wouldn't let him.'

She smiled and hutched into the curve of Jo's shoulder. He felt her hair flicking against his face and remembered how often he had carried Josie like that – her black hair drifting in the wind.

'No, I wouldn't have whapped her. It was him I was gunning for.'

He had said it lightly but he knew that, if he had caught them then, it would have come to shooting. He had been that crazy. For a moment he clung to Emmie-May as if she had rescued him.

After a while the land fell away a little and they could make out a straggle of buildings – a street – a whitewashed church. The Doctor's new motor-buggy was parked outside the saloon. Jo nodded to the storekeeper, out front with a broom. He wondered what folks would think of him riding into town, dust to the eyeballs and a strange kid in his arms. He hitched his horse by the Sheriff's office and said to Emmie-May, 'Just sit here for a while, I'll tell them about your mom and then we'll go find the Pastor.'

She nodded and sat on the veranda, cradling the doll.

Jo pushed the door. The office was thick with tobacco

smoke but empty except for a grizzled officer, half-asleep under his newspaper.

'Well, Jo! I haven't seen you in a while. What's the story?'

'I was riding way out on the plain when this kid just popped up under my nose. I never knew there was a homestead out there. Seems she lived there with just her mother and the mother had taken a fall. I went back to the house with her. The woman's dead – fell from the loft. I brought the girl into town to see who'll take her. Old man Andersen, died this winter, was her grandpa, she says.'

Sheriff Olafsen scratched his stubble and looked Masterman over.

'You'd better bring her in, Jo, but I think you lost your bearings out there. There ain't been no-one at Andersen's place in thirty years. Last time I rode that way there was hardly a post left. Your little girl's sun-struck, maybe.'

Jo shrugged and went to fetch the child. The veranda was empty so he went down to where the horse was tethered, looked up and down the street. There was no sign. He called to the storeman who was still sweeping his steps:

'Hal! You seen where the kid went? The one I brought into town? I left her here sitting as nice as pie and now I can't see a sign of her.'

Hal straightened his back and peered at Jo.

'I didn't see no kid with you, not riding nor sitting. You okay, Jo?'

Jo was already running to the church – *that* was where she would go. He found the Pastor, sickle in hand, clearing an overgrown corner of the churchyard.

'Pastor, do you know where Andersen's buried? Died last winter? I brought his granddaughter into town. She's wandered off. I thought she'd be here.'

'Andersen? Not this last winter. Not in my time, I think, Jo. The last Andersen I know of is here.' He knocked down some weeds to reveal a weathered stone. Jo read:

> In memory of Kurt Andersen, died December 21st, 1880, aged 75, and his only daughter, Mary, died June 19th, 1881, aged 32.
> *And the lost shall be found in Christ.*

Jo shook his head,

'Well, whoever she is, she still may come here. Look out for her. I have to go with the Sheriff. Her mother's lying dead back there.'

But, as he returned to the office, he had begun to doubt that she was.

On the railroad fence-post Jo's neck-cloth fluttered but beyond it the prairie ocean stretched unbroken, featureless except for ripples of silver as the wind bowed the grasses. Here and there the dint of a 'cat's paw' showed and vanished. If there was a high, soft singing, perhaps it came from the fence-wires that ran above the rails. If Emmie-May danced with her doll through the grass, she left no more trace behind her than did the sunlight.

Ants

Alice Baynton

On the east coast of Northern Cyprus is the city of Gazimagusa. Stretching from turquoise sea through into countryside is Varosha, ghost city, a wide expanse of dead ground that slashes Gazimagusa in two, dividing Greek Cyprus from the TRNC.

The beach is lined with dilapidated tower blocks, each floor a wind tunnel with empty windows, the odd spear of glass still clinging to its frame. The high rise streets soon give way to clusters of hollow homes and rusting cars. Constantly chattering cicadas replace the hum of traffic. Nature has reclaimed this part of the city. Diesel, frying food, hot garbage bins; the olfactory abuse of the city pauses for thought at the fence. This land belongs to the aromas of stone dust, animal waste and fennel.

Grass suffocates, tall enough to hide a grazing donkey; a playground for stray cats. Jagged holes in roofs stick out tongues of purple jacaranda.

A dirty white church. Only one window remains. Saint Frances stands still in a wood, drenched in birds of all colours.

Four worn stone steps lead to the always open door. At the top of these is Mustafa. The stone of the church seems whiter against his gleaming black boots. Motionless in camouflage and a pair of knock-off Ray-Bans, his hands sweat around his rifle.

Through the baking midday quiet, he hears a car rumbling up the road towards him. Nobody uses the useless green line road these days, except tourists. Sure enough, as the car rounds the bend and slows to a stop, it's a shiny blue Peugeot. Leather skinned parents step out of the front, and three overweight, pink nosed children out of the back. They peer through the fence, the mother raising a camera. Mustafa sighs before taking the few steps to the wire and testing his rusty English.

'No picture. Notice!' he points with the business end of the rifle to the crooked but obvious sign three feet from where they stand. The family apologise and scramble back into the car. The children look out of the rear window as they drive away. Mustafa turns back to the church and takes his place by the open door.

Inside the church is dark and cool. A tear of sweat creeps down the side of his nose, past the corner of his mouth, over his chin and hangs there for a moment, as if steeling itself for the drop. It is dislodged with a tiny shake of the head. It falls and lands on an ant next to his boot. The ant drowns in what must feel like a ton of salty oil. Mustafa watches, not moving a muscle. He barely breathes as a rushing flood of memory overwhelms him.

A day as searingly hot as this one, ten years ago.

Two eight-year-old boys running along the green line road. They had found a deflated football beside the crisp corpse of a hare. They took a few moments to decide which to play with. There were so many things they could do with each of them. They opted for the football. Now they booted it back and forth, clouds of sandy dust kicking up a lot higher than the un-bounceable rubber.

Mustafa kicks the ball, the browned, tired trainer of his right foot splitting a little more at the toe.

'Gooooaaaaaaaalllll! David Beckham!'

Mehmet stops running, looking at him in disgust.

'No, I'm David Beckham today, you're Ryan Giggs.'

'Don't care. Ryan Giggs is better anyway.'

Mehmet shakes his head, sticks out his tongue and turns away. He catches sight of a hole in the fence. There is a tensing of the back of his neck, the sudden stillness of acute interest. Mustafa runs to join him and sees the gaping hole through to forbidden territory. With the wordless eloquence of best friends they glance at each other, nod, step through.

Moving through this unknown landscape, they make for an island of corrugated iron roof and greying walls. Paddling through the grass is slow progress, toes catching on bricks and stones, tripping, slipping their way to the promise of a cool dip in the shade. They reach the house, met with a blank wall-face. Negotiating their way around the building, their unthinking hands drag along behind them. The surface of parched stone and whitewash is irresistibly crumbly to the touch.

Rounding the corner they come into an abrupt dirt clearing, a snake coiled in the middle of the bare space. Mustafa plucks a long strand of grass and moves forward. A pain in his shoulder stops him. Mehmet has it pinched between thumb and forefinger, knuckles white with the strain.

'My father says this kind is the soul of an evil man. The devil sends them back as snakes. You can tell because the black in their eyes is round like people.'

'That's not true!' Mustafa laughs, thinks for a moment, and adds; 'Your father smells like a goat.'

'Only because he works at the Mezbaha. At least *he* has a job. And anyway, it is true because when did you ever see a snake with round eyes?'

Mustafa considers this. He stares at the snake, the unthreatening colouring and size making him scoff. Cynicism wrestles with the fear of getting the evil eye. He decides it isn't worth the risk, throws the grass stalk down and steps back.

'I'm bored anyway. Look, there's a church!'

They regard the bell tower they can see above the trees. It does look like a church, so they move toward it, neither admitting, but both glad that they will be protected from the evil eye.

The door stands open, hinges rusted beyond movement. The two boys step inside and pause, their eyes taking a few seconds to adjust to the cool dark. At the end of the short aisle, Jesus hangs from the wall. The right half of his face chipped off. The remaining half wears an expression of pitiful longing, the nails through his palms being the least of his worries when compared to this perpetual solitude.

'Why did they do that to their god?' Mehmet asks, wiping a flat palm up his nose.

Mustafa shrugs. 'Infidels.'

'Yeah, I guess. Look!' Mehmet, so easily distracted, has seen a black line of movement on the stone floor. The ants stride in unison, well trained soldiers focussed completely on one distant aim. The two boys start gathering together stones, twigs, broken tiles and bits of plastic.

One stone placed in front of the line, forcing the ants to change direction. They march left, to be met with a ridge of blue plastic.

Left again, a tile.

Turning right, a Fanta bottle.

Right again, a plank of wood on its edge.

Another left, a cracked and sticky lighter.

The ants are turned off course by the two boys, again and again, but never break ranks. With intense concentration, precise and careful placements, a maze takes shape.

Confusion begins suddenly, the ants hit just one too many obstacles and the whole system of command implodes in an instant. They divide into groups, dithering between this way and that. Next, individuals break from the groups and run over and on top of each other. The boys turn to each other, grinning. They feel like giants. They swell with power and control. Kings of the ant world.

A few minutes pass in silent concentration, before it breaks up and boredom floats like tissue in water. Mustafa stretches his neck, peering up at the flaking paintings on the ceiling.

'Does God still live here if nobody comes?'

Mehmet shrugs.

*

The sun is bashing down on the steps now, reflecting off the white-ish church walls. Mustafa takes his cap off, scrubs up his oil-dark hair and shakes away the sweat.

His mind wobbles. After the barrage of memories, reality feels like walking out of the movie theatre into daylight.

He checks his watch.

4.00pm.

He has been standing at these steps for eight hours. Soon his relief will be here. To stand still in a forgotten part of the country.

He stretches out his neck by twisting it first left, to the quiet crack of a vertebrae, then to the right. His body follows ever so slightly and he glances into the church. A few tiles and rocks lie on the floor, too ordered to be accidental.

Over adolescence and his two years in the army, living along the green line and spending his days within it, he has stopped questioning. His time is spent standing, sweating and thinking. He has come to his conclusion. Nothing changes. Ten years, ten days, the same empty buildings. The same half starved cats piss and mate in the same places. The same snake skin bunched in a clearing, fossilising.

God doesn't live here any more.

Author biographies

Elizabeth Baines' stories have been published widely in magazines and anthologies, and her collection, *Balancing on the Edge of the World*, is published by Salt, who also publish her two short novels, *Too Many Magpies* and *The Birth Machine*. Her work is included in two previous Honno anthologies, *Power* and *Laughing, Not Laughing*. She has also written prizewinning plays for radio and stage, and she is the runner-up in 2014's International Short Fiction Journal prize.

Alice Baynton has written stories since she could hold a crayon. Born and raised in an idyllic valley out in the wilds near Aberystwyth, she honed her craft and spent a lot of time with her cat. She studied Creative Writing at Liverpool John Moores University before travelling in South America and going to live in New Zealand for a year. She is currently half way through her Masters in Creative Writing at the University of Manchester, living nearby in Cheshire. Despite all of the moving around, her heart is still very much in mid-Wales, and she has to return home for regular top ups of Welshness. She has had two short stories published by the small, independent *Tranquillity Publishing*, is a contributing editor for the online travel magazine *Eventus*, and despite having yet to begin her first novel, she can feel it brewing.

Caroline Clark (65), originally from the Midlands, has lived in Aberystwyth since 1978, when her husband came to work there. She has mainly been active in community theatre since coming to Wales – as an administrator, performer, director and wardrobe mistress. She has always written poetry and more recently short stories, which have been published in various anthologies including Honno's *Written in Blood.* She regularly reviews books for the Gwales website. In recent years, while being a fairly housebound carer, she completed a novel and has plans for another. She is also working on a collection of poems relating to the local landscape and history.

Pam Clatworthy was born in Rumney, Cardiff and educated at the village school, which was an exciting place during WW2 as air raids disturbed lessons and talented, married women were allowed to return to teaching. She went on to Gowerton Girls Grammar School and finally trained as a teacher. She moved to Cumbria where she now lives and has written for *The Countryman*, *Daily Telegraph*, *Guardian* and has had short stories and poetry broadcast on regional radio. Pam is married with two children and five wonderful grandchildren who all love a 'cwtch' from time to time.

Chrissy Derbyshire is an author, folklorist and storyteller based in Cardiff. Her first book, *Mysteries*, was published in 2008. She has since had several stories, poems and essays published in magazines and anthologies, and is a regular speaker at The Mercian Gathering.

Eileen Dewhurst has lived and worked in North Wales for more than twenty-five years. She loves reading and writing, being with friends and family, making a bit of music now and then and, most of all, being outside walking with the dog.

Maria Donovan grew up on the Dorset coast and lived for some years in Holland before moving to Wales in 1997. She likes languages, peace and studying history. Her first collection of short stories, *Pumping Up Napoleon*, is published by Seren.

Gillian Drake was born in Barry and now lives in Swansea. Her two books for teenagers were both published by Pont; other published work includes short stories, articles and poetry. Gillian is a graduate of Aberystwyth University, and gained an MA in Creative Writing from Swansea University in 2005. She has worked in the voluntary sector in areas as diverse as archaeology, mental health and education.

Melanie C. Fritz was born in south-western Germany in 1982 and only came to Wales in 2006 to study at the University of Glamorgan and to learn a bit of Welsh. She has enjoyed making up and writing down stories ever since she was taught the alphabet and, to date, she has published two novels in her native German: *Weltmeister im Handtuchwerfen* in 2010 and *Chaos im Kessel* in 2014. She lives in Pontypridd, a place that inspires her somehow.

Jacqueline Harrett is a former teacher and lecturer with a passion for oral storytelling. She has had articles published in the *TES* and her resource book for teachers, *Exciting Writing*, won the UKLA author award in 2007. Throughout her teaching career she tried to inspire others to engage with the written word.

Jacqueline was born in Northern Ireland and has two grown-up children. She has lived in Cardiff for more than twenty years with her long suffering husband, a mad cat and a tortoise called Speedy.

After years of inflicting her writing on her colleagues on an in-house magazine, **Nic Herriot** finally let loose her creativity in 1995 when she completed an MA in Creative Writing at Trinity Carmarthen. Her ideas come from family, friends and adventures that happen in the real world. All her family have left home, to save themselves the embarrassment, except her poor wife, who is waiting for her passport to come through. Nic wrote this story as part of her campaign to show that there are good care homes out there.

Suzy Ceulan Hughes is a writer and translator. *Mad Maisy Sad* is her third short story to be included in a Honno anthology.

Rona Laycock was born in Bangor, North Wales. Over the years she has taught in schools and colleges in the UK, Pakistan, Tunisia and Egypt, established and run a 'helpline' for a local BBC radio station, and trained emergency response volunteers for NGOs and local authorities. She has an MA and PhD from Swansea University where she studied with the late Nigel Jenkins, who was an inspirational mentor. She runs creative-writing courses and literary events in and around Gloucestershire, where she now lives with her husband, David. Her work has been published in various national and international magazines and anthologies.

She is the editor of writing magazine, *Graffiti,* and her first poetry collection, *Borderlands*, was published in the form of an audio CD in 2009 by Music Masters Ltd and Cole's Press.

Jo Mazelis' collection of stories *Diving Girls* (Parthian, 2002) was short-listed for Commonwealth Best First Book and Welsh Book of the Year. Her second book, *Circle Games* (Parthian, 2005) was long-listed for Welsh Book of the Year. Her novel *Significance* was published by Seren in September 2014. She lives in Swansea.

Sue Moules has published three poetry collections: *The Moth Box* (Parthian), *In The Green Seascape* (Lapwing), and *The Earth Singing* (Lapwing). She also published a joint collection *Mirror Image* (Headland). She is a member of the poetry performance group Red Heron.

Sue has been published widely in literary magazines including *Poetry Wales, New Welsh Review, Planet, Ambit, The North, Orbis, Ambit* and *Roundyhouse*. Her work has also appeared in many anthologies: *On My Life* (Honno), *Exchanges* (Honno), *Poetry Wales 25 Years* (Seren), *The Ground Beneath Her Feet* (Cinnamon), *The Voice of Women in Wales* (Wales Women's Coalition), *Of Cake and Words* (Cledlyn), *A Star Fell From Orion* (Peter, Bridge and Stephen), and *Poetry From Strata Florida* (Carreg Ffylfan Press). She was featured as the first Honno poet of the month in July 2012 and will be Honno poet of the month again in July 2014.

Siân Preece was born in Neath and studied English Literature at the University of Wales, Swansea. She has lived in Canada and France, and in Scotland, where her first story collection, *From the Life*, was published by Polygon. Now based in Cardiff, she took an MA in Creative Writing at Cardiff University, and in the following year won the 2010 Rhys Davies Short Story Competition with her story 'Getting Up'. She writes stories, drama and abridgements for Radio 4, and is currently working on a novel and a second story collection.

*

Penny Thomas is publisher at Firefly children's Press and fiction editor at Seren. She lives in Cardiff with her two children.

The Wish Dog is the third collection of short-stories that **Stephanie Tillotson** has edited for Honno, two in collaboration with Penny Thomas. Herself a published playwright, poet and short story writer, Stephanie worked for many years in television, radio and theatre production. She now lives in Aberystwyth and is writing a doctoral thesis at Warwick University on Shakespeare in performance.

More from Honno

Short stories; Classics; Autobiography; Fiction

Founded in 1986 to publish the best of women's writing, Honno publishes a wide range of titles from Welsh women.

All Shall Be Well

A quarter of a century's great writing from the women of Wales

Edited by Penny Thomas & Stephanie Tillotson
A wonderful and absorbing collection of writing by Welsh women taken from the fiction and non-fiction anthologies published by the press over the last quarter of a century.

ISBN: 9781906784331 £9.99 (paperback)
ISBN: 9781906784461 £14.99 (hardback)

Cut on the Bias

Stories about women and the clothes they wear

Edited by Stephanie Tillotson

An anthology of short stories that explores the intensely personal relationships women have with what they wear.

"*Reading these stories is better than shopping!*"
Nicola Heywood-Thomas

ISBN: 9781906784133 £8.99

Coming up Roses

Stories of Gardens and Life

Edited by Caroline Oakley

Stories for the Green Fingered: From birth to death, horror to hilarity – a collection of stories for gardeners at home and away.

"Crime, romance, loss, haunted tales... this collection has it all."
Lynda's Book Blog

ISBN: 9781870206938 £7.99

Written in Blood

Edited by Lindsay Ashford and Caroline Oakley

From bodies buried under the patio to old ladies with enviable inheritances, and from a Chandleresque pastiche to police procedurals.

"The sheer variety and craft of these stories makes for a very satisfying read while reminding us of the drama underlying apparently innocent lives"
The Short Review

ISBN: 9781906784010 £7.99

A Time for Silence

Thorne Moore

1933: Gwen's duty to her husband John has a terrible price. Now: Sarah becomes obsessed with restoring her grandparents' ruined farm. Two women, one dark secret...

"...after a few short chapters I was hooked... Piece by piece, she builds these women's lives until they sneak into our affections. The most chilling part of Thorne Moore's skill is the way that she represents evil."
Helen Tozer, sideline jelly

ISBN: 9781906784454 £8.99

Inshallah

Alys Einion

With twin boys only months old, Amanda arrives in Saudi Arabia to live with her husband Mohammed. Her new life is strange and confusing...

"The compelling story of one woman's extraordinary journey... by turns gripping, provoking and vividly sensory"
Tiffany Atkinson

ISBN: 9781909983083 £8.99

Eden's Garden

Juliet Greenwood

Sometimes you have to run away, sometimes you have to come home: two women a century apart struggling with love, family duty, long buried secrets, and their own creative ambitions.

"*A great romantic read and also a very atmospheric, ingenious mystery.*"
Margaret James, *Writing Magazine*

ISBN: 9781906784355 £8.99

The Wooden Doctor

Margiad Evans, edited by Sue Asbee

First published in 1933, this is the gripping story of an obsessed adolescent, her alcoholic father, and a strange, seemingly incurable disease.

"*..a gripping, tempestuous novel, intense, beautifully written with an emotional range that sweeps from passion to tenderness.*"
Dr. Jeni Williams

ISBN: 9781870206686 £8.99

A Welsh Witch

A Romance of Rough Places

Allen Raine, edited by Jane Aaron

'They say she's a real witch,' says Goronwy Hughes' grandmother, warning him of Catrin Rees, the heroine of *A Welsh Witch*. The sea-side village of Treswnd has elected Catrin as its scapegoat, shunning and stoning her as a witch.

"*Dramatic and well observed...its warm depiction of Wales adds another dimension to its value.* "
Steven Lovatt, *New Welsh Review*

ISBN: 9781906784652 £10.99

ABOUT HONNO

Honno Welsh Women's Press was set up in 1986 by a group of women who felt strongly that women in Wales needed wider opportunities to see their writing in print and to become involved in the publishing process. Our aim is to develop the writing talents of women in Wales, give them new and exciting opportunities to see their work published and often to give them their first 'break' as a writer. Honno is registered as a community co-operative. Any profit that Honno makes is invested in the publishing programme. Women from Wales and around the world have expressed their support for Honno. Each supporter has a vote at the Annual General Meeting. For more information and to buy our publications, please write to Honno at the address below, or visit our website: www.honno.co.uk

Honno, 14 Creative Units, Aberystwyth Arts Centre, Aberystwyth, Ceredigion, SY23 3GL

Honno Friends

We are very grateful for the support of the Honno Friends: Jane Aaron, Annette Ecuyere, Audrey Jones, Gwyneth Tyson Roberts, Beryl Roberts, Jenny Sabine.

For more information on how you can become a Honno Friend, see: http://www.honno.co.uk/friends.php